SS PANZER BATTALION

January 1940 ... the coldest winter within living memory and the phoney war still paralyses the Western front, but at the Adolf Hitler Kaserne a new battalion of SS troops trains for a mission so secret that it is known only by its *Wehrmacht* code name, Zero. The Vulture – Major Horst Geier – is the only man who knows that the objective is the key Belgian fortress guarding the junction of the River Meuse and the Albert Canal – the most impregnable fort in Europe, which must be taken if Hitler's SS Panzer troops are to turn the flank of the Maginot Line.

SS PANZER BATTALION

SS PANZER BATTALION

by

Leo Kessler

Dales Large Print Books
Long Preston, North Yorkshire,
BD23 4ND, England.

British Library Cataloguing in Publication Data.

Kessler, Leo
    SS Panzer battalion.

    A catalogue record of this book is
    available from the British Library

    ISBN   978-1-84262-503-3 pbk

First published in Great Britain in 1975 by Seeley, Service & Co.

Copyright © 1975 Futura Publications Ltd.

Cover illustration © Carlos Pino by arrangement with
Temple Rogers Artists' Agents

The moral right of the author has been asserted

Published in Large Print 2007 by arrangement with
Eskdale Publishing

Dales Large Print is an imprint of Library Magna Books Ltd.

Printed and bound in Great Britain by
T.J. (International) Ltd., Cornwall, PL28 8RW

'Blood is our beer, steel our meat.
Nothing we fear, we know no defeat.
Better dead than red.
SS Assault Battalion Wotan, march –
  enemy ahead!'

TRANSLATOR'S NOTE

For the sake of simplicity and better understanding the normal Army ranks have been used throughout this translation instead of the Armed SS designation of Kuno von Dodenburg's original. For those, however, who may care to work out the exact ranks of the members of SS Assault Battalion 'Wotan', the following table gives the most important ones:

SS

A. Standartenführer
B. Obersturmbannführer
C. Sturmbannführer
D. Hauptsturmführer
E. Obersturmführer
F. Untersturmführer
G. Sturmscharführer
H. Hauptsscharführer
I. Oberscharführer
J. Scharführer
K. Unterscharführer
L. Rottenführer

M. Sturmann
N. SS-Mann

GERMAN ARMY

A. Oberst
B. Oberstleutnant
C. Major
D. Hauptmann
E. Oberleutnant
F. Leutnant
G. Stabsfeldwebel
H. Oberfeldwebel
I. Feldwebel
J. Unterfeldwebel
K. Unteroffizier
L. Gefreiter
M. Oberschutze
N. Schutze

BRITISH ARMY

A. Colonel
B. Lt-Colonel
C. Major
D. Captain
E. Lieutenant
F. 2nd-Lieutenant
G. Regimental-Sergeant-Major
H. Sergeant-Major
I. Quartermaster-Sergeant
J. Staff-Sergeant

K. Sergeant
L. Corporal
M. Lance-Corporal
N. Private

And among all the many SS units that saw action in the war there was none more battle-hardened, more brutalized and more ruthless in their devotion to war and violent death than Kuno von Dodenburg's *SS Assault Battalion Wotan.*

SECTION ONE:
THE ROAD TO BATTLE

'Gentlemen, you realise the importance of our task. If we fail we hold up the whole advance of the Greater German Wehrmacht!' *Captain Geier, C.O. 2nd Company, Wotan to his officers, 8 May, 1940.*

CHAPTER ONE

'Stillgestanden!'

Two hundred pairs of army boots crashed to attention as one. As the troop train which had brought them to Eifel started to draw away from the platform, Lieutenant Schwarz reported to the officer who had come from the battalion to meet them. 'Draft from Sennelager! All present and correct, *sir!*' Schwarz gave the First Lieutenant an immaculate salute and stared at him fiercely.

First Lieutenant von Dodenburg, whose chest bore the black wound medal and the ribbon of the Iron Cross, acknowledged it with the casual air of the veteran.

'Thank you, Lieutenant,' he said to Schwarz. He turned to the draft. 'When we leave the station, we sing; and when I say sing, I mean it. So that the locals can hear that we're not the Army, but the SS!'

Schulze, the draft's comedian, nudged his neighbour and indicated the peasants staring at the soldiers in open-mouthed awe, 'Them dummies look as if they've got to be told to come in out of the rain. Bet they don't even know what the SS is!'

'Quiet there!' Schwarz yelled, as he

15

prepared to march the draft out of the station.

'A song – *one, two, three!*' the draft's 'first voice' commanded as they swung into the Street of the SA. Two hundred lusty young voices crashed into the first verse of the *Horst Wessel Lied*. Fat-bellied local Storm Troopers snapped to attention as the noise of National Socialist Germany's second national anthem filled the narrow cobbled street. But the undersized peasants who lined the pavements did not react. They stared at the eager young giants who stamped by them on the worn cobbles as if they were invaders from another planet. 'Look at 'em,' Schulze's neighbour whispered, breaking off in the middle of 'their brittle bones shall tremble', 'they don't like the SS. Half of 'em have got French blood in them anyway. That's why we're here. To kick the Frenchies out of the Maginot Line, and teach this lot what it means to be German.'

Schulze grinned and winked at a pretty, dark-haired girl, who blushed and looked away hurriedly. 'No,' he whispered. 'The Führer hasn't sent us down here to fight, lad. He wants his SS to put a bit of German beef into the local girls. We're not here to fight – we're here to…'

'One more word from you,' a harsh voice cut in, 'and I'll have your name in my book

16

quicker than you can pull out your filthy tail!'

They swung round a corner, past the onion-towered Catholic church, and saw ahead of them the red-brick pile of the Adolf Hitler Barracks, their new home.

Kuno von Dodenburg clasped the hilt of the dagger of honour which Reichsführer Himmler had handed to him personally upon his graduation from the Bad Toelz SS Officers' School two years before. *'Parade march!'* he bellowed, as he marched under the wooden arch which bore the motto OUR HONOUR IS OUR LOYALTY.

Behind him the irrepressible Schulze echoed the command. 'Parade march – the captain's got a hole in his arse!' But his words were drowned by the steel-shod clash of two hundred pairs of jackboots hitting the concrete of the parade ground. At their head von Dodenburg could not suppress a shiver of pleasure at the sound. He knew he was behaving like a recruit at his first parade. After four years in the SS he should be able to accept it for what it was – a drill movement. But he couldn't. For him the crash of heavy boots striking the ground in perfect unison symbolised the new Greater Germany, marching from victory to victory. And the men at whose head he had the honour to march were the élite of the German *Wehr-*

macht – the Black Guards; still raw admittedly and in need of more training, but already assigned to the élite of the élite – *die Leibstandarte*, the Adolf Hitler Bodyguard Division.

'Morning, soldiers!' Captain Geier yelled as soon as von Dodenburg had reported to him.

'Morning, Captain!' came back the traditional reply.

Captain Geier, their new company commander, was a small thin officer, whose monocle and light grey breeches, with their cowhide inlet, marked him clearly for what he was – a regular officer who had transferred from the Army to the Armed SS because promotion was better. His mouth was a thin line, as hard as his icy-blue eyes. But it was not the mouth nor the eyes that drew the draft's attention – it was the Captain's nose, a monstrous abomination of flesh which would have been laughable on another man. But laugh at Captain Geier and one lived to regret it. After von Dodenburg had recovered from the chest wound he received in the Polish campaign of the previous autumn and had been posted to Geier's company, he soon learned that the captain was not a man to be fooled with.

'Stand at ease!' Geier commanded. He slapped his riding cane against the side of his highly polished topboots. 'Soldiers, my name is Geier, which I am told, aptly suits my appearance.' He stroked his monstrous nose, as if to emphasise his point, but no one laughed.

'At present, as you can see, my rank is that of a captain. But my father was a general and before this war is over, I promise you I shall be General Geier too.' He pointed his cane at them challengingly. 'And do you know how I shall do it?' He answered his own question in the thin rasping Prussian Army voice that all the regular *Wehrmacht* officers von Dodenburg had known, seemed to affect. 'I shall do it on your backs and, when you die, on the backs of those who come after you – as they undoubtedly will.'

Next to von Dodenburg, Schwarz's sallow face broke into a faint smile, as if Captain Geier were joking. But von Dodenburg knew his company commander was deadly serious. The previous September Geier had led a full company of the pre-war Body-guard into the Battle of Bzura in Central Poland. With great dash he had taken his objective and become the first officer in the whole of the *Wehrmacht* to win the Iron Cross, First Class. The Führer himself had presented the decoration. But it had been gained at the cost of a shattered shoulder, which made it impossible for Geier to carry anything heavier than a riding cane in his

19

right hand, and the loss of three-quarters of his company. The draft was here to replace those dead, nearly a hundred and twenty of them.

'You have now joined the premier regiment of the Armed SS,' Geier went on. 'The battalion to which you belong from this moment onwards is the best within that regiment and it goes without saying that the best company in that battalion is my company. *Do you understand that?*' His eyes searched their ranks for any sign of weakness or doubt, but there was none. For the young men who faced him were the best that National Socialist Germany could produce – devoted followers of the Führer, whose last six years in the Hitler Youth and the Work Service had been one long preparation for this proud moment when they finally joined the formation which bore the bold white legend 'Adolf Hitler' on the arm of its field-grey uniform.

'I cannot tell you the details of your assignment here in the West,' Geier continued. 'All I can tell you is that you will have exactly three months to prepare for it. But when we march west and show those damned Tommies and Poilus how to break the Olympic record in running back to where they came from, I want you men of the Second Company to work like the devil for me. I have the medal.' He tapped his chest with the riding cane. 'That's enough tin for the time being until the Führer, in his wisdom, decides that he'll cure my throatache.' The Captain was referring to the Knight's Cross which was worn round the neck and was jokingly referred to as 'throatache'; yet there was something unpleasantly cynical about his reference to the decoration as 'tin'. 'This time I want something more tangible. I want to come out of the next campaign in the West as commander of this battalion. Do you understand?'

He let the words sink in. 'I do not ask you to love me. I do not ask you to respect me. All I ask from you is that you obey my orders with unquestioning obedience.' His eyes swept their ranks once more. 'And God help any one of you, soldier, NCO or officer, who fails to do exactly that.' The Vulture's voice rose harshly. 'Soldiers I welcome you to SS Assault Battalion Wotan!'

CHAPTER TWO

The duty NCO blew his whistle and banged open the door. '*Aufstehen!*' he yelled at the top of his voice as if he were on the parade ground and the sleeping men were a hundred yards away, and not ten feet. 'Hands off cocks – on socks!' They woke up immediately. In their four months in the SS the draft had learned long ago that it didn't pay to linger. At the door the duty NCO in his tracksuit, whistle hanging round his neck, hands on hips, stared grimly while they dropped on to the polished floor from their wooden double-decker beds.

'*Ausziehen!*' he commanded when they were all out of bed.

Swiftly they pulled off their old-fashioned issue nightshirts and stood naked and shivering in the cold air that came through the wide-open door.

The duty NCO mustered them contemptuously, not even granting them the comfort of movement. Finally he snapped, '*Lueften!*' They pulled down the blackout shutters and opened the big windows. Ice-cold air streamed in. The soldiers' teeth chattered.

'Sergeant,' said Schulze, 'I think mine's going to shrink away altogether in this blizzard. Do you think I could report sick.'

The duty NCO's expression did not change. 'You may Schulze,' he said. 'But I warn you that the MO was on the booze last night. He's got the shakes this morning. But if you want him to sew it back on again for you...' he shrugged and left the rest of the sentence unfinished. 'All right now – shower!'

They scampered for the showers at the end of the room. As each one entered, he raised himself on the fixed bar and did the obligatory three pull-ups. A moment later the duty NCO turned on the icy water at full blast. 'Rotten sadist!' someone yelled, but the NCO had already moved on to rouse the inmates of the next room. The first day of training in 2nd Company, SS Assault Battalion Wotan had begun.

'My name is Butcher – butcher by trade, butcher by name and butcher by inclination,' the red-faced Sergeant-Major bellowed at the men of the 2nd Company, standing rigidly to attention in the centre of the square. His rat-trap of a mouth snapped open again and his voice, oiled by countless cheap cigars and litres of beer, roared across the parade ground and bounced off the walls two hundred metres away. 'Believe you me, nothing in this world would give me greater pleasure than to make mincemeat of you heap of wet sacks! Do you get that?'

Sergeant-Major Metzger, 2nd Company's senior NCO, glared at the new arrivals. Standing there as if some God of War had planted him in the middle of the parade ground to show pale-faced recruits what a real soldier looked like, he ran his eyes along their ranks. They flicked from soldier to soldier, looking for a button undone, a helmet set at a wrong angle, a dull belt buckle – anything which he could use to demonstrate his well-known ability to 'turn a man into a sow', as he was wont to boast to his drinking cronies in the NCO's wet canteen.

To his disappointment Metzger found nothing that would grant him an opportunity to give expression to one of his celebrated outbursts of temper. Almost reluctantly he got down to the business of the day. 'All right then,' he bellowed, 'we'll get on with it! *Stand at ease!*'

Automatically their left feet shot out. Metzger placed his hands behind his back and began to raise himself up and down on his toes. It was a movement he had seen in an old film about the First World War; the gesture had pleased him and he had adopted it as soon as he had been promoted to corporal five years before. In his considered opinion, it intimidated the average SS man and he was pleased to note now that the eyes of the front rank followed his up-and-down movement with slightly scared expectation.

'You think you're already soldiers,' he began. 'But you're not. You're a bunch of chimney-sweeps, run wild, a lot of rooting sows, a collection of slack arseholes.' He ended his litany of abuse with his favourite phrase; 'A bunch of shit!'

'Now it is my duty and those of the NCOs to attempt to turn a bunch of shit like you into something approaching soldiers.' He raised his hand as if to ward off their protests. 'I know, it is almost tempting fate to make the attempt. Who in his right mind would ever think it possible, save perhaps the Butcher? But I have promised the CO that I will try.' His voice rose from the mock sentimental to its true fury.' 'And heaven, arse and twine, God and His Son protect anyone of you wet sacks who dare let me down! *I'll cut his cock off! God help me, so I will.*'

SS Assault Battalion Wotan's assault course was one kilometre long – the brainchild of some ardent follower of the Marquis de Sade. A narrow plank suspended ten metres above the ground, a drop into a nettle-filled ditch, its walls sheer mud, a twenty metres crawl under knee-high barbed wire, a wooden-plank wall fifteen metres high, a terrifying lunge for mud-slippery ropes an arm's length away, a breath-catching plunge into an icy, fast-flowing stream and finally five rounds rapid fire at moving targets.

The Butcher, coolly standing at the end of the course, stop-watch in hand, looked at the mud-stained, chest-heaving company in naked contempt. 'Ten minutes,' he sneered, 'what do you think this is – a shitty girls' school obstacle race or something? Even those wet sacks of the First Company can do the course in nine-fifty and everybody knows they're a bunch of warm brothers. Too much playing with it at night, that's what it is. Five against one! Now I bet if one of them poxy whores from the house behind the barracks – yes, your old sergeant-major has got eyes in his head. He wasn't born yesterday – were to lift up her skirts and show you dirty men her drawers, you'd be chasing after her quick enough!'

'You know what his problem is, mate?' Schulze said to his neighbour. 'It's his missus. She's got pepper in her pants and the Butcher can't give her enough.'

'Did you say something, soldier?' the Butcher snarled.

'Yessir,' Schulze answered dutifully. 'I said, perhaps we aren't trying hard enough!'

Metzger snorted. 'Well, at least one of you rooting sows knows what I'm talking about. All right, let's do it again.'

Groggily, their eyes glazed with exhaustion, their heavy packs biting into their shoulders, they lined up to begin the course once more.

A skinny blond soldier with thin artistic hands hung on to the steel stake driven in the side of the plank wall. In vain he tried to lever himself up to the next one, but his muscles would not pull him any further. He was beat like the rest of the 2nd Company. This was the fourth time they had been over the course. The man hung like a piece of limp meat, tears streaming down his muddy face.

'You drunken crab, get up that wall!' the Butcher yelled, 'or do you want me to come over there and help you up? By God, you'll regret it, if I do!'

'I can't, Sergeant-Major!' the soldier gasped. Behind him Schulze put up his hand and pushed with all his strength. The soldier almost shot over the top of the wall.

'Who told you to do that, soldier?' the Butcher screamed, his red eyes bulging.

'My hand slipped, Sergeant-Major,' Schulze answered. 'Muddy as hell up here.'

Before Metzger had time to reply, he heaved himself up and over. The next moment he was dropping into nothing, his hands catching the wet rope just in time.

They lay face downwards in the frozen grass like dying men. The sweat poured from their bodies in spite of the cold and the backs of their drill uniforms were black with moisture. 'I'd like to get him alone at the back of the barracks,' someone gasped. 'I'd cut his bleeding balls off with a blunt knife.'

'You and whose army?' Schulze asked with dry contempt. 'Give it a couple of months and you'll be as bad as that bastard your-self.'

'Nobody could ever get that bad,' the

youth who had been stuck on the wall said. His hands were a bloody mess where he had ripped his nails on the wall. 'Not bad like that; it's impossible. I don't...'

A sharp voice cut into the conversation. 'Sar'nt Major, what kind of a damned piggery is this!'

'*Sir!*' the Butcher bellowed at the top of his voice. They turned in sudden alarm as the Sergeant-Major gave Lieutenant Schwarz a tremendous salute and made his report: 'Second Company, Assault Battalion Wotan on assault course. One hundred and seventy-two men present. Nothing special to report, *Sir!*'

The sallow little officer looked up at the NCO. 'Nothing special to report, did you say, Sergeant-Major?' He pointed at the sweat-lathered men sprawled on the ground exhausted: 'And what do you call that?'

The Butcher tried to bluster, but Schwarz cut him short. 'An SS man is an *élite* soldier, Sergeant-Major. He can't afford to loll about like those chaps in the Army can. I'm afraid you're molly coddling them – you're too soft on them. Now trot off to my car and get the box you'll find behind the seat.'

Like an obedient recruit, glad to get out of the way before the matter developed any further, the burly Sergeant Major 'trotted off' to carry out the Lieutenant's order, while the latter passed the time by making the exhausted company do a few press-ups – using the left hand only.

While the company formed a circle round him, their chests heaving with the fresh exertion, Schwarz opened the wooden box. He took out a small metal object and straightened up again. 'A British Mills bomb, vintage 1916, captured in Poland last September. This,' he touched the metal pin, 'is the firing pin. If I pull it out, the bomb will explode within four seconds.'

Calmly and deliberately he pulled out the pin but kept his hand round the lever it released. 'If I were to drop this now,' he said, 'every one of you within ten yards' range would be killed or severely wounded. Now, I'd like you all to take ten paces to the rear.'

Mystified and not a little scared, the men shuffled back the required distance. Schwarz waited patiently.

'In Bad Toelz, we had a little game that was perhaps a little silly, but I think it did separate the men from the cowards. It went something like this. We took a grenade and place it on the crown of our helmets.' He suited the action to his words. Suddenly the faces all around him went pale, as the men guessed what he was going to do next.

'Thereupon we released the pin.' The lever went whining through the air. Schwarz did not seem to notice. But his voice was a little strained as he said, 'Now one has about three seconds left. The trick is to keep one's head perfectly straight. If you tremble, you have no head left to...'

The explosion drowned the rest of his words. A vicious red-yellow flame spurted momentarily from the top of his helmet. Red-hot slivers of razor-sharp steel hissed through the air in all directions. The men of the 2nd Company hurled themselves to the ground.

Schwarz, standing rigidly to attention in their midst, looked down at their sickly-white faces maliciously. '*Soft tails!*' he sneered. 'Frightened by a little bit of a firework, half of you look as if you've wet your knickers!'

He gave them a few seconds to get back to their feet again. With an impatient sweep of his pale hand he knocked the remaining fragments from the scorched top of his helmet and turned to the Butcher, whose face was also drained of colour. 'Sergeant Major,' he snapped, businesslike again, 'I want you to issue grenades to the first twenty men and then stand them twenty metres apart.' The Butcher, recovering himself quickly and obviously relieved that the officer did not expect him to participate in this crazy exercise, shouted at the men in the front rank: 'Didn't you hear what the officer said? What's wrong with you? Have you been eating big beans or something? Get the lead out of your arses – you, you and you pick up those grenades! Come on now.'

Reluctantly the first men moved over to the wooden box to receive one of the deadly little eggs. But they were fated not to go through with the exercise. Suddenly the cultured voice of First Lieutenant Kuno von Dodenburg broke into the proceedings. 'Lieutenant Schwarz,' it said softly, 'I wonder if I could speak to you for a moment?'

Schulze breathed out an audible sight of relief.

'Schwarz,' Kuno von Dodenburg snapped, trying to check his anger, 'the purpose of training is not to kill your men but to prepare them for battle in such a manner that they *won't* get killed.'

'What do you mean?' Schwarz asked angrily.

'I mean, comrade,' von Dodenburg said softly, using the familiar term in order to appear not to be pulling rank on the other man who was probably only a year younger than he was himself, though he had been in the Black Guards less than a year, 'that that business with the grenade was damn stupid and might have ended unfortunately.'

'To make an omelette, you have to crack eggs,' Schwarz persisted.

'Even in training there have to be casualties. The weak, the cowards, the unfit must go by the board so that the brave may survive on the battlefield.'

'There are no brave men on a battlefield,' von Dodenburg said, knowing that he was sounding like his father at his worst. 'There are only fools and skilled soldiers.'

'Then how did you get that bit of tin?' Schwarz asked, pointing to his black wound medal.

Von Dodenburg grinned. 'For keeping my mouth shut when my company commander made a balls up of things in Poland and then helping him to get out of the shit he had landed himself in.'

'I must remind you, sir, that although you are my superior officer,' Schwarz said with sudden icy formality, 'there are certain things which I am bound by my honour as an officer of the Armed SS and my membership of the National Socialist Party to report.' He lowered his voice a little. 'Perhaps it would be wise of you to remember, Lieutenant von Dodenburg, who my uncle is.'

Von Dodenburg's face creased in a look of utter disbelief as he stared down at Schwarz. When he spoke, each word was like the drop off an icicle. With the authority of ten generations of Prussian cavalry officers behind him, he snapped icily: 'Schwarz you are a garden dwarf, a nasty little garden dwarf! In addition, you are a complete arsehole! I know exactly who your uncle is. *Now what are you?... And stand to attention, man when I speak to you!'*

Like a green recruit, Schwarz standing rigidly to attention, said: 'I am a garden dwarf, a nasty little garden dwarf...'

His voice trailed away.

'Louder!' von Dodenburg bellowed, pushing his face into Schwarz's.

'And in addition,' Schwarz whispered miserably, 'I am a complete arsehole.'

'How right you are. Now get those men back into their billets and tell that fool of a sergeant-major to report to me within half-an-hour that they have had their cuts and bruises treated and are being properly fed. I hold you responsible for him, Schwarz. Do you understand?'

'Yessir.'

'Then don't stand there, man! Get on with it!'

Schwarz ran off as if he were trying to break some record.

CHAPTER THREE

But in spite of von Dodenburg's intense dislike of Schwarz's concepts of training which went directly against those advocated by Brigadegeneral Berger, the real founder

33

of the Armed SS, he knew that a certain amount of dangerous training had to be chanced. In Poland he had seen how a single German tank had panicked a whole Polish infantry company by simply driving over the first enemy foxhole. The Poles had scrambled frantically from their holes, flung away their weapons and fled in panic.

Although the Vulture had still not revealed their mission to his officers – 'my dear von Dodenburg, you will learn that unfortunate piece of news early enough, believe you me,' had been his answer to von Dodenburg's query on the subject – he knew it must be against the French or English. And both had tanks, lots of them. Von Dodenburg therefore decided that although it was highly dangerous he would have to train the 2nd Company to face up to a tank attack on their positions.

The morning was beautiful, with the winter sunshine sparkling on the whitened roofs and the birds singing, as they marched out of the town up to the training ground on the hill, where the ancient Mark I tank was already waiting for them, its black-clad crew stamping their feet on the snowy ground to keep warm.

Von Dodenburg halted the company and strode across to the sergeant of the *Panzerwaffe*, who reported smartly enough, though his eyes under the big black beret were fixed anxiously on the shining young faces of the

SS men chattering in the background. 'One Mark I tank, crew three, present, sir!'

'Thank you, Sergeant.' Von Dodenburg acknowledged his salute and then as casually as he could, he asked: 'Everything all right and ready to go, Sergeant?'

'Yes sir,' the tank man said.

Von Dodenburg strode back to his men. 'In front of you, you see a Mark I tank, all six and a half tons of it. A nasty looking object indeed, you must agree, especially if you're infantry without any anti-tank weapons at hand. Now let us assume that it was a Tommy *Valentine* or one of the new French *chars* and it was advancing on you, what would you do?'

No one volunteered any information, until Schulze put up his hand like an overgrown schoolboy.

'Yes, Schulze?'

'Run like hell, sir,' he said cheekily.

Von Dodenburg smiled. 'The Gods take care of fools, the ancient Greeks said, but let us say that you didn't want to run away. Instead you preferred to stand and fight heroically, or perhaps you'd hurt your foot and couldn't run,' he added for Schulze's sake.

'You'd dig a hole, sir,' a soldier suggested.

'Exactly.' He pulled down the cuff of his elegant grey glove and glanced at his wristwatch, 'and you've got exactly fifteen minutes

35

to do just that.'

The company groaned. They had obviously been expecting the order. It was part of the old Army game that they had come to know only too well in these last few months. 'Anybody here studied music? Yes. All right then, come over here and help to move the piano. Any of you men a plumber? Good, then go and clean out the officers' latrines.' Grumbling good-humouredly they got out their entrenching tools and began to hack at the iron-hard earth below the snow. Von Dodenburg watched for a moment, then he undid his own spade and started to dig his own foxhole, while behind them at the tank the crew smoked nervously.

Von Dodenburg gave them five minutes. 'Just so that you'll get the lead out of your lazy arses,' he yelled, poised over the pile of earth he had already raised, 'it might interest you to know that in exactly ten minutes from now, that tank will roll over your foxholes – each individual hole. And if you are a coward like me, you'll dig like hell!'

He bent down again so that he didn't have to see the look of consternation and fear which shot into their eyes. Suddenly a heavy silence fell over the training ground, broken only by the harsh breathing of the digging men and the scrape of their shovels on the hard earth, as they worked like men possessed.

Kuno crouched in his hole. The tip of his helmet was level with the edge of the trench, and the fifteen minutes were up. He rose again and shouted. 'Time! Everyone down now! Sergeant, start up your sledge!'

There was no answering laughter from the men crouching in the holes.

The Sergeant threw away his cigarette end. Below in the dark interior the driver pressed the starter button and the 120 HP engine burst into life with an ear-splitting roar. The Sergeant kicked the driver's left shoulder, and the latter pulled back the left tiller bar. With a rusty squeak the tank lurched forward and began to rattle over the uneven ground to the line of brown holes, which looked like the work of some gigantic mole.

As Kuno had agreed upon with the sergeant, the tank headed for his foxhole first. The roar was above him now, blotting out the light. The young officer, as pale and as frightened as his men, huddled at the bottom of his hole. His lungs were filled with the stench of diesel. His eardrums threatened to burst with the tremendous roar. Instinctively he closed his eyes like a little child and tried to blot it out from his mind. The heat of the exhaust seared the back of his neck, then it was gone. Cautiously he poked his head above the edge of his hole, a wave of relief surging through his body. Behind the tracks, throwing up dirt and pebbles in their wake, head after head was beginning to pop up.

At last the tank came to a halt. The Sergeant turned and wiped the sweat from his face. Von Dodenburg could see his anxious gaze running from hole to hole and the relief mirrored clearly on his face at each new head which popped up. But from three holes there was no sign of life. He thought of his own criticism of Schwarz a couple of days before and clambered hastily from his hole, but before he had reached the blank holes, Schulze, his face black with mud, rose from his slit trench and roared in a fair imitation of an old Regular Army sergeant: 'Beg to report, sir, three casualties!'

Von Dodenburg stopped in his tracks.

Schulze grinned cheekily, his teeth a dazzling white against the black mask. 'Two fainted,' he added, *and one shit hissen!*'

'Thank you, Schulze.'

'There's just one thing, sir,' Schulze added.

'Yes?'

'What would have happened if that tank had swivelled round on its tracks on the top of our holes? Don't you think the Tommies'll be smart enough to know that that's the way to break in the sides of a foxhole?'

'Schulze,' von Dodenburg said slowly, 'you're too damn smart to be allowed to run around loose.'

'That's what my mother always used to say, sir,' Schulze said, in no way put out by the veiled threat.

That same evening Kuno von Dodenburg called the big Hamburger, who was half a head taller than himself, to his quarters. Schulze squeezed through the narrow doorway and snapped to attention.

Von Dodenburg left him standing for a moment while he pretended to busy himself in front of a mirror. When he looked up he caught Schulze grinning at his back in the mirror. 'What are you grinning for like a monkey up a stick?' he rapped.

'Nothing, sir. I was just born with a mug like this,' Schulze said. 'Some people are born with mugs that only a mother could love. Others have faces that you'd like to spring at with your naked arse, if you'll forgive me speaking good German? And then there are others who have happy faces – like me.'

'Happy faces,' von Dodenburg commented. 'Looks more like dumb insolence to me.'

'At your command, Senior Lieutenant,' Schulze barked with undue formality, the smile wiped off his face as if by some invisible hand.

'Insolent sow!' von Dodenburg said without any anger. 'All right, Schulze, relax.'

'Relax – military or civvies, sir?' Schulze asked.

'What's the difference?'

'I could write a book about it, sir.'

'I understand – civvie.'

The shoulders slumped immediately. The line of the chin softened and with a quick twist of his thumb and forefinger he snapped open the catch of his tight collar.

'Why don't you strip completely?' von Dodenburg asked sarcastically.

'I would, sir, but my mother said I should never take my clothes off in front of strangers.'

Von Dodenburg ignored the remark. 'Tell me, Schulze,' he said, 'how the devil did you ever get into Assault Battalion Wotan? Somehow or other – to put it mildly – you just don't look the type.'

Schulze was in no way offended. 'Well, sir,' he began slowly, 'when the Greater German Reich realised what a threat those Polacks were and the Führer, in his far-seeing wisdom, decided that we must invade Poland in order to protect ourselves, I decided the time had come to do my bit.' He licked his big lips.

Kuno von Dodenburg looked up at the massive Hamburger, realising that Schulze was pulling his leg, yet knowing that the latter was too cunning to allow himself to get caught. 'Go on,' he said, 'with the story of our patriotic struggle for Fatherland and Führer.'

'Well, I wouldn't put it exactly like that, sir,' Schulze objected, his face a study in mock seriousness. 'You see there was a girl involved. She was a member of the Beauty and Belief Organisation. But in this case she wasn't all believe and no beauty.' He made a quick female shape, sweeping his calloused hands through the air. 'Built like a brick shit-house, she was, sir, if you'll forgive my good German once more. Well, with a girl like that I couldn't have joined the Coastal Artillery or the Supply Service. She wouldn't have opened her pearly gates for anybody who served in a rearline outfit like that. No sir, it had to be the SS or nothing. Naturally I knew I wouldn't be accepted. I had a reserved job in the docks. And besides I've always had a weak chest.' He coughed hollowly and rapped his chest. 'My poor mother often said she wondered how I ever survived with all the colds I had as a kid. Anyone in his right mind could see I wouldn't measure up to the high standards of the SS.'

'Naturally,' von Dodenburg agreed.

'Not that sow of a MO though. He counted my teeth as if I were some old nag, sniffed under my armpit to check if I were a Yid and grabbed hold of my short arm and made me cough, as if you were supposed to use it to clear your throat and not for a bit of the other. Then he passed me fit, and I was in the SS. Me, the son of old Red Schulze of

Barmbek who would have turned over in his grave if he'd have known I'd gone to serve under Adolf – excuse me, sir, the Führer, Adolf Hitler. So here I am, the lowest form of life in Assault Battalion Wotan.'

'And the girl?'

'*Her!* It turned out a lot different than I thought, sir. On my first leave, I came home all dressed up like a dog's dinner in my number one uniform, sports medal, my monkey swing, the lot and took her out to the *Cafe Vaterland* for a drink and a dance. It's been my experience that when you've got 'em dancing a bit, with your knee between their legs in the tango, you have 'em halfway on their backs already. But when it came for her to open the pearly gates back in her flat there were tears and protests and lots of fuss and feathers, but none of the other.'

'Why not?'

''Cause she didn't like men, it turned out. It was girls and bits of rubber. Can you imagine it, sir? A girl preferring that to a real bit of meat! I bet the rubber's ersatz too.'

'Undoubtedly,' von Dodenburg said and suddenly burst out laughing.

Schulze watched him without the suspicion of a grin on his face, as if he were studying some rare form of life. Finally he said with unusual politeness, 'If I may draw the Senior Lieutenant's attention to the fact, the Senior Lieutenant requested me to come

42

to his quarters for some particular reason.' Then the respectful tone disappeared and his voice assumed its normal thick waterfront accent, which most of the Southerners in 2nd Company could not understand. 'Besides, the Bavarian hillbilly who shat himself this morning is going to spring a round of free beer in the wet canteen in ten minutes' time.'

Von Dodenburg shook his head in mock despair. 'All right, I need a general dogsbody – driver, runner, etc., and I thought of you.'

Schulze's eyes lit up. 'A batman, sir?' he asked enthusiastically. 'My old man was a batman in the War and all he ever got was a dose of pox in Brussels.'

'No, I didn't mean my batman. Captain Geier does not believe in such animals. You'll still carry out your normal company duties while we're in training, but as soon as we go on active duty status, you'll revert to me as a personal orderly. What do you say?'

'Sounds all right to me, sir. There's just one thing. If I could come over and have a look-see if everything was all right in your quarters in the morning, then I'd be prepared to accept your offer, sir.'

'So that you won't have to do the morning fatigues?'

'No, sir! I've been on the craphouse ever since I came here, sir. And in the early

43

morning those thunderboxes fair turn my guts over!'

'All right, Schulze, you're on. You're certainly not as dumb as you look.'

CHAPTER FOUR

Sergeant-Major Metzger had already come to that conclusion himself, though it had taken him a little longer to do so than it had Lieutenant von Dodenburg; but then everything took a little longer with the Butcher. As his cronies in the NCOs' wet canteen were wont to say: 'Sergeant-Major Metzger doesn't know his ear from his arsehole most of the time.' Nevertheless he had been smart enough to work his way up to the most coveted NCO position in the company.

As far as the Butcher could see, Schulze was an excellent soldier. But somehow he lacked that 'animal seriousness' which the Sergeant-Major expected from his men. He saluted like a Prussian grenadier, but there was always something akin to sarcasm in his eyes. His parade march was the best in the whole battalion, but as soon as he relaxed, his gait was as sloppy as any Ami cowboy. And although Schulze always seemed polite enough, the Butcher had a sneaking feeling that the ex-docker was pulling his leg when he spoke to him. As he told his cronies in the wet canteen, 'You can say what you like, *meine Herren*, but I think that fly shit of a sailor is pulling my pisser half the time.' In the notebook which replaced his brain, Sergeant-Major Metzger made a little black cross against the name 'Schulze, Richard' and promised himself he'd keep an eye on the man; it was a promise which boded no good for Schulze, Richard.

It was a cold grey afternoon. There was snow in the air and above the firing range the clouds were leaden. But Schulze did not let himself be deflected by the weather or by the pain in his groin. He'd made too much of a pig of himself the night before in the big house behind the barracks. 'Man, you go at it like Blücher and his cavalry,' the blousy whore had complained afterwards. 'At least you could take off your dirty boots!' 'I can't, my little cheetah,' he countered. 'I might slip in altogether, if I took 'em off.'

Carefully he adjusted the sight of his '08'. It was the third time it had slipped this afternoon. He squeezed the trigger. The butt smacked against his big shoulder. Up at the butts, the chessboard appeared.

Lieutenant Schwarz, who was in charge of the firing party, grunted his approval. 'Another twelve, Schulze,' he said. 'Where the devil did you learn to shoot like that!'

'A natural talent, sir,' Schulze said, not turning round and knowing that he could afford this act of *lèse-majesté*, since a whole group of NCOs and SS men had formed up in a semi-circle behind him.

Schulze tucked in the butt again, feeling the weapon like an extension of himself. He closed his left eye and took careful aim. Around him the spectators held their breath, mentally going through the movements with him.

'Another twelve,' Schwarz cried. 'How the devil do you do it?' But he did not attempt to answer his own question. 'Listen Schulze,' he said enthusiastically, 'trot off to the gunnery sergeant and get yourself another ten rounds on my authority. Sergeant-Major Metzger holds the battalion shooting record – and we're gonna break it.'

'Did anyone mention my name, sir?' It was the Butcher himself. He had come up with the 'goulash-cannon', which would provide 2nd Company with its midday meal that day – pea soup and sausage.

Schwarz, who found nothing wanting in the Sergeant-Major's 'national socialist attitude', as he called it, wagged his finger at the NCO. 'It looks as if this green beak here'll break your record, Sergeant-Major, if you're not careful.'

The Butcher forced a smile while Schulze

'trotted' over to the gunnery sergeant to sign for a further ten rounds. 'Good luck to him, sir,' he said with apparent casualness. 'But even a blind chicken can find its corn sometimes.'

'Perhaps you're right. Maybe it's a fluke. We shall see.'

But the noisy protests of Schulze's comrades, who knew that he had already won the marksman's lanyard back at Sennelager, made the Butcher uneasy. 'Cut it out!' he bellowed. 'Let's have a bit of quiet in the knocking shop.'

Obediently they lapsed into silence as Schulze stretched himself out on the firing pad. All he needed now was a lousy five and he would have broken the Butcher's record. Schulze took very careful aim, the butt tucked into his shoulder tightly, his finger curling round the trigger. There was a dead silence. He could almost feel the couple of hundred pairs of eyes fixed on his back. Slowly, very slowly he began to squeeze the trigger. Behind him there came the sudden clatter of a canteen falling to the ground. The single shot went whining through the air, wide of the target.

At the butts the red flag began to wave back and forth. 'Fanny's drawers,' Lieutenant Schwarz said sympathetically. 'Hard luck, Schulze!'

The Butcher picked up his canteen.

'There goes my pea soup,' he grunted. His big, red face beamed at Schulze, who was rising to his feet, slapping his knees free of dirt, his eyes livid with anger. 'Not bad, Schulze, not bad at all. We'll make a marksman of you yet. But you've still got to learn a bit if you want to compete with an old soldier.' Throwing Schwarz an immaculate salute, he turned to get himself some more soup before the men could get their greedy fingers on the biggest sausages.

Schulze watched him go in silence, but at that moment he swore a silent oath. One day Sergeant-Major Metzger would pay for what he had just done – one day very soon.

That day came sooner than Schulze had expected. One week after the incident at the range, the whole battalion was suddenly alerted to move to Trier, the ancient provincial capital, to parade before the Führer himself. Hitler would be making a stop-over there on his way back from an inspection tour of the West Wall.

'Our battalion will lead the parade,' the Vulture explained to his officers. 'The Führer has expressed a special wish to see Wotan.' He turned to Schwarz, and took out his monocle to polish it. Von Dodenburg, watching his bent head, somehow had the feeling that Geier did not want them to see the look in his eyes at that moment. 'Oh and by the way, Schwarz, your uncle will also be in the Führer's party. He has asked the battalion commander to request my permission to let you go that night. Naturally, I gave it forthwith.'

Schwarz could not quite conceal his pride at the mention of his famous uncle. 'Thank you, sir,' he said. 'I appreciate your kindness.'

Schwarz was not alone in his appreciation of the opportunity offered by the Führer's visit – Schulze saw that it gave him the chance he had been waiting for to get into the Butcher's quarters.

On the morning of the parade, he reported sick when the duty NCO woke them at six. The NCO, who was known as 'hole-in-the-arse' because he had received a painful wound in his backside during the Polish campaign, looked at the naked Hamburger suspiciously. 'Are you lead-swinging, Schulze?'

But Schulze's pale face and the shadows under his eyes seemed to show that he was not trying to get out of the Führer-Parade. 'I've been on the thunder-box half the night, Corporal,' he said weakly. 'It's the trots. A couple of times I thought my back-teeth were going to go as well.'

'Hole-in-the-arse' made a note in his book. 'All right, you can report sick. But woe betide you if you're trying to pull my pisser!'

Senior Staff Doctor Horch, whose doctoral thesis on '*Methods of Establishing Non-Aryan Racial Types by Body Smells*' had gained him an immediate commission into the SS, was too busy to concern himself overly with the miserable-looking Hamburger. 'Thin shit', he diagnosed, using the Germanic expression instead of the effete Greek word 'diarrhoea'. 'Light duties and charcoal tablets and raw apples twice a day. Report to me *cured* tomorrow morning.'

'Yes, Senior Staff Doctor!' Schulze said weakly.

Horch made a note in his records. At present he was trying to cure all illnesses with natural remedies; he'd even tried prescribing geranium leaves in the ears for toothache. When he was finished with his researches, he would present his findings to Reichsführer Himmler himself. Only one thing worried him about his project, however. The most common complaint among the young men in the Wotan Battalion was gonorrhoea, against which the natural remedy of peppermint tea and raw garlic did not seem to be very effective.

Outside Schulze spat out the wad of evil-tasting tobacco which had produced the required symptoms, but the trick had been worth it. He was one step nearer his aim.

A blond-haired eighteen-year-old, racked by a terrible cough, which Doctor Horch was treating with infusions of camomile tea, had been detailed to clean out the Metzger apartment. Schulze waited till they were outside the duty NCO's office, then taking out a five mark note, pressed it into the boy's hand. 'Here,' he said, 'go over to the wet canteen, buy yourself a bottle of rum, mix yourself a couple of stiff ones with hot water and sugar and it'll do your chest more good than all the crap that cracked pill-roller is giving you.'

The surprised youth accepted the note gratefully. 'But what about the Butcher's apartment?' he asked after a prolonged burst of coughing.

'Leave that to me, old lad,' Schulze said, picking up the carpet-beater which the duty NCO had given him for the job. 'I'll take this.' He grinned. 'I'll give Frau Metzger's carpets the best beating they've ever had.'

Sergeant-Major Metzger's fat, blonde wife was sitting on the sofa in the bare little living room of their apartment in the block opposite the barracks when he knocked on the door and was told to enter. On the little table at her side, a half-empty glass of Kirsch was placed within reaching distance. On her ample bosom she had balanced an open box of liqueur chocolates and was picking at them with plump white hands, licking her red-painted fingers after every one. 'What do

51

you want?' Lore Metzger said, without looking up, her attention concentrated on the sticky chocolates.

'I've come to beat your carpets, Mrs Sergeant-Major,' Schulze snapped in his best military manner, standing at attention. He knew the type. In Hamburg they called them 'green widows': suburban housewives with no children, who spent their days drinking, smoking and playing with their nails, bored with the world, their husbands and themselves; their lives were empty of anything that could make them believe that they were desirable attractive woman.

'Can't you see that it's raining outside?' she said, still not looking up. 'You can't beat carpets in this weather.'

'Is it, Mrs Sergeant-Major?' Schulze played stupid. 'I didn't notice.'

'Some of you soldiers are so dumb that you have to be told to get in out of the rain,' she said scornfully. She reached forward to pick up her glass of Kirsch and gave him a generous glimpse of her white well-developed bosom, which threatened to bounce out of her low-cut peasant blouse at any moment. 'And the bitch knows it too,' he thought to himself.

But his broad face did not reveal his feelings; it was a mask of obedient stupidity, the archetype of the dumb common soldier.

'Well, don't stand there like a spare prick

at a wedding,' she snapped, draining the glass. 'Sit down a minute. It might stop soon.'

'I'll give you spare prick at a wedding, madam,' he said to himself. But when he spoke his voice was full of humble gratitude for this act of great benevolence. 'Thank you, Mrs Sergeant-Major, you are very kind.'

He sat down on the very edge of the chair, his back rigid, his knees close together like some timid schoolboy visiting his headmaster. She refilled her glass and for the first time looked at him properly. Deliberately he let his eyes follow the movement of the liquid from the bottle into her glass. The look worked.

'All right,' she said, 'you don't have to look like Jesus on the cross. Get yourself a glass. Top right in the cupboard there.'

He rose hesitantly. 'May I, Mrs Sergeant-Major?'

'Of course, I wouldn't say so otherwise. And for God sake, stop calling me Mrs Sergeant-Major!'

After that thing went off in great style, as Schulze had planned they would; after all he had played out this little scene a good half-hundred times in the last ten years since he had had his first experience at the age of fourteen with the mother of his best pal at school.

They talked about the weather. Then it

was the SS. Another glass of Kirsch. Carefully he steered her around to her own life with the Sergeant-Major. Undoubtedly it must be a lonely life being married to such an important but busy man as Sergeant-Major Metzger? It was. 'If you only knew how lonely,' Lore Metzger sighed with all the repressed desire of her fat bored romantic soul. Another Kirsch.

As if by accident, he touched her fat knee as he handed her the glass. She shivered with desire. He gave her a few moments more, then placed his big muscular arm round her shoulders, as if it were the most natural thing to do in the world. Through the thin blouse he felt her firm flesh, hot and slightly damp. He put his hand inside her blouse and toyed with her nipple.

She closed her eyes and sighed: 'What must you think of me?'

He made as if to take his hand away, but she grabbed it quickly and placed it back on the erect nipple. He shrugged and planted his lips on hers. Their tongues met and intertwined like two snakes. Over her naked shoulder he caught a glimpse of the Butcher sitting proudly on a white horse in his pre-war black uniform. Schulze winked at the photograph cheekily, then turned his mind to the job in hand.

A few minutes later her brassiere and panties lay on the carpet, as she tip-toed to the door, clad only in her black silk stockings, and locked it. Carefully, so that she wouldn't alarm her neighbour by the sudden noise, she lowered the shutters.

He had her the first time on the couch. Afterwards she scampered away giggling to the bathroom. As she ran by, he slapped her ample bottom with his big hard hand, more with pleasure than revenge, and said to the photograph: 'One!'

The next time he had her in the matrimonial bed. She objected a little, but not much. For him the squeaking of the springs and the wooden protesting of the frame were like music: the tangible accompaniment to his act of revenge. Two!

The third time he made her do things that 'I've never even done for the Sergeant-Major – and I've been married to him for ten years. I never even seen things like that in the books he confiscates from the soldiers – the dirty pigs!'

Schulze knew he needed to play with her no longer. He grabbed her by her long blonde hair and forced her down on him. Thereafter there was only pleasurable silence. Three!

It was three o'clock in the afternoon when he left her apartment, the unused carpet beater under his arm. She was asleep on the rumpled bed, a look of complete satisfaction on her fat face. It was matched by the one on Schulze's face, though there was a hint of malice in his smile.

Slowly and a little painfully – he had a faint nagging pain between his legs, which he guessed, wrongly, could only come from one cause. He made his way over the road towards the entrance to the Adolf Hitler Barracks, where the trucks were beginning to unload the men returning from the parade.

'You,' a voice bellowed.

Surprised, he turned round and snapped to attention, the carpet beater held at his side like a rifle.

It was Sergeant-Major Metzger in full uniform. 'I thought you were sick?' he said accusingly. 'Where have you been with that?' He indicted the carpet-beater.

'The MO gave me light duties, Sergeant-Major,' Schulze snapped in his best military manner. 'I was over at your apartment beating the carpets for Mrs Sergeant Major Metzger.'

The Butcher's surly manner relaxed a little. It had been a long strenuous day in the rain at Trier and he was tired. All he wanted now was to get his clothes off and have a drink. If Schulze had done the heavy work, perhaps Lore wouldn't be too tired this evening. It would be a change. After all, love was the bread of the poor man, he told himself, using a phrase he had picked up from some film or other. 'Well, did you beat them properly? My wife's particular, you know.'

'You can rely on me, Sergeant-Major,' he answered promptly. 'I gave the carpets a real going-over. They'll stay beat for a good few days to come.' He saluted and passed on quickly before the NCO could see the look of triumph in his blue eyes.

CHAPTER FIVE

In Trier that same evening Lieutenant Kurt Schwarz also experienced a moment of triumph when he met his uncle again after six years and the great man decided to spend the evening with him. He jerked an elegant hand at the door and said in a high, nasal voice. 'Out, Müller!' Obediently the shaven-headed Chief of the Gestapo got to his feet. 'You, too, Nebe.' The Head of the Criminal Police followed his colleague to the door. There they turned and snapped to attention. *'Heil Hitler, Obergruppenführer!'* they bellowed in unison.

Their chief stated at them. 'Tonight,' he announced as if he were making an official statement, 'I am going to talk politics to Kurt here. Then we are going to get gloriously drunk. And after that' – he stuck his thumb between his two fingers obscenely – 'we're going to find what this Godforsaken papist dump has to offer a man in the way of pleasure. Understood?'

'*Understood, Senior Group Leader,*' they bellowed. They had understood all right. Senior Group Leader Reinhard Heydrich, the head of the Reich Main Security Office, feared throughout Germany as 'Hangman Heydrich', was going to go on one of his celebrated binges, and they were thankful they were not being asked to go along with him; for in his cups, the tall blond SS General, with the delicate hands of a violinist (which he was) and the ice-cold eyes of a killer (which he was too,) was even more dangerous than normal.

When they had gone, Heydrich swung his gleaming boots on to the table, pulled over a bottle of cognac and poured himself a stiff drink. He shoved the bottle towards his nephew. 'Help yourself, Kurt,' he said.

Without waiting for his nephew, he rapped 'no heel taps' and downed the contents in one gulp. 'Push the bottle over,' he said and in the same breath: 'Well, how are you liking your service in Assault Battalion Wotan?'

Kurt, still a little awed by his famous uncle, sketched in a few details about the 2nd Company.

Heydrich listened attentively, drinking all

the while, apparently not even noticing that he was doing so. 'And the spirit among the soldiers?'

'Excellent.'

'And the officers?'

Schwarz hesitated, and then shrugged. 'There are some who are not hard enough,' he began.

'Senior Lieutenant Kuno von Dodenburg for example?' Heydrich said softly. He laughed at the expression on his nephew's face. 'Our informers are everywhere, my dear Kurt,' he explained. 'I could tell you some fine things about your little Captain Geier too. It is not only horses he likes to ride, believe you me. But I won't; it might shock your sensitive young soul. You see, Kurt, my police force embraces every aspect of the nation's life. I need information about everyone so that I can correct and direct the people's thoughts. It is only in this way that we can eliminate everything foreign and therefore destructive from the national thinking. The police as a purifier and the educator of the Great German Nation – that is my aim!' For a moment his eyes sparkled fanatically. Then he took another deep drink of cognac and swung his boots off the table top. 'But come on, young Kurt, let us not waste any more time. We shall see what the most catholic city of Trier, old when Rome was young as the locals boast, has to offer two high-spirited soldiers.'

As he waited for his big black Mercedes to pull up outside the hotel, he nudged Kurt Schwarz familiarly. 'Did you hear the one about the two nuns and the blood sausage?' he began, and launched into the first of many obscene jokes that the young Lieutenant would hear from his uncle that night.

'Close the streets, the SS marches.'

The storm-columns stand at the ready.'

Reinhard Heydrich stumbled and nearly fell in the dark hotel corridor.

'Shush Uncle – everybody's sleeping!' Schwarz urged. But the Head of the Reich's Main Security Office was past caring.

'Let death be our battle companion. We are the Black Band,' he howled drunkenly.

Finally Schwarz managed to get his uncle through the door of his suite and sighed gratefully as he closed it behind him with the heel of his boot. He let Heydrich slump into an armchair and opened his shirt at the neck. Somehow he'd got the blind drunk Chief of Germany's security system back to his hotel without incident. He had never spent such a boozy evening in his whole life, even during his cadet days at Bad Toelz. His uncle had been drinking solidly for six hours: cognac, gin, whisky, wine – everything and anything alcoholic. His stomach must be made of cast iron.

Suddenly Heydrich lurched to his feet. 'Got to piss,' he said drunkenly. With one hand stretched out in front of him like that of a blind man, he staggered to the bathroom.

Schwarz slumped in the chair he had just vacated and stretched out his jackbooted legs in front of him gratefully. God, what wouldn't he give now for a bed! He felt he could sleep for the next forty-eight hours without waking. Sleepily he closed his eyes. His chest began to rise and fall gently.

But Lieutenant Schwarz was fated not to sleep much that night. Suddenly a shot rang out. He sat bolt upright in his chair. The noise had come from the bathroom. He jumped to his feet and ran across the room.

His uncle was staring at his reflection in the shattered mirror, one hand holding the basin, the other holding his service pistol which trembled dangerously. Slowly he grimaced at himself in the broken glass. 'Now I've got you, you Jewish scum!' he said slowly.

Schwarz looked at him aghast. His uncle looked completely sober. 'What did you say?' he asked.

Heydrich turned round. 'Jewish scum, I said.' He laughed, but there was no mirth in his laughter.

'What *do* you mean, Uncle?' Schwarz persisted.

'It is perfectly simple, my dear Kurt,' Heydrich said, his voice clear and unslurred now. 'Your father and I are Jewish. Your grandmother was called Suess, Sarah Suess, and I am sure your studies in racial anthropology and genealogy at Bad Toelz will tell you what that means – the Heydrich family is Jewish!'

'Jewish?'

Heydrich looked down at his nephew mockingly. 'Yes, we are both Yids.'

CHAPTER SIX

Slowly the winter of 1939–40, the hardest in living memory, gave way to spring. The black poplars which bordered the Adolf Hitler Barracks began to turn green. Now when the NCOs weren't looking, the 2nd Company men slowed down. In winter they had moved quickly of their own volition, to keep warm. But spring was here and it was getting too warm to do everything at the double as Sergeant-Major Metzger wanted. 'Heaven, arse and twine,' they grumbled, 'he'd have you go for a crap at the double if he had his way!'

The spring also seemed to have brought an end to the long *sitzkrieg* in the West. At 5.20

am precisely on 9 April, 1940, the troopship *Hansestadt Danzig* sailed into Copenhagen, filled with German troops, to be directed to its berth by General Kurt Himer, the head of the German task force, who had arrived in the Danish capital two days before in civilian clothes. It was all too easy. Denmark surrendered before the day was out at a cost of twenty German casualties.

Norway was next, though this time the enemy resisted more strongly. The headlines of the Führer's own newspaper *Voelkische Beobachter* and the Rhenish *Westdeutsche Beobachter*, which were available in the troops' day rooms, were full of news of the battles around Narvik, Trondheim and Fornebu, and the heroic deeds of General Dietl's Bavarian mountain troops.

New equipment started to pour into the Adolf Hitler Barracks that month, indicating to the men of the 2nd Company that their baptism of fire would come soon. Their old trucks and horse-drawn transport disappeared to be replaced by gleaming new half-tracks. Every platoon received one of the deadly MG 42 machine guns with its air-cooled mechanism that enabled it to fire 80 rounds a minute. And on the very day that morning drill was interrupted so that they could hear the special announcement from the Führer's Headquarters that Narvik had fallen they received their first consignment of flame-throwers. The men of the 2nd Company looked at each other significantly, as the demonstration team from the Army's Special Weapon Office began to unload their deadly freight. 'Close combat weapons,' they whispered among themselves. 'This is going to be a close combat job!'

The burly NCO in charge of the three-man demonstration team, allotted to the 2nd Company, tapped the round pack of fuel on the soldier's back. 'This is the core of the team,' he said heavily. 'But it's damn sensitive, believe you me. One slug just glancing off that thing and it's goodnight Marie.'

The 2nd Company laughed dutifully, but without conviction.

'So, what do we do?' The NCO answered his own question. 'We give the man with the flame-thrower the best protection we can. That's what numbers two and three are for.' He pointed to the two infantry soldiers, heavily laden with assault rifles and grenades, standing like two plates from an Army instructional manual.

He cleared his throat. 'All right, that's the objective, that bunker.' He pointed to the mock pillbox some fifty metres away. 'How do we take it?'

Without waiting for an answer, number two started to crawl forward towards the bunker from the left, a smoke grenade clasped in his right hand. Number three, in his turn, dropped to the ground, feet spread apart at the prescribed angle and began to blaze away with blank ammunition at the pillbox's firing slot.

Suddenly the man with the grenades held up his hand. The number three stopped firing at once and the man threw his grenade. There was a sharp crack like a dry twig breaking underfoot on a hot summer's day and the pillbox was enveloped in thick grey smoke. The rifleman jumped to his feet and placed himself at the side of the man with the flame-thrower, lining himself up on the number one as if it was some kind of drill movement.

The NCO blew his whistle. They doubled forward into the smoke, which was clearing rapidly. The rifleman fired from the hip as he ran to the left of the man with the flame-thrower, but the observers from the 2nd Company noted he was careful to keep a little behind. A second later they saw why.

The number one pressed the trigger of his terrible weapon. A hissing tongue of flame shot forward. It wrapped itself around the mock pillbox. Little bubbles of paint spurted up on the woodwork. The air was filled with the stink of burned wood and scorched grass.

The NCO looked at them in silence. Even after two dozen such demonstrations, he could not quite overcome the mood of awe which descended upon him after the flame-thrower had done its work. 'If that had been the real thing, any living creature within twenty metres would have had its lungs collapsed through lack of oxygen – and anything hit by the flame itself would have been burned away to one half of its size. Look like little black pigmies they tell me,' he added thoughtfully, almost as if he were talking to himself.

The arrival of the flame-throwers was followed by intensive house-to-house fighting, carried out in one of the local hamlets, hurriedly evacuated at the battalion commander's order for this purpose. Time and again they practised the same old drill for taking a house – a burst of sub-machine gun fire along the line of the windows to make its occupants duck, the door flung open, the stick grenade lobbed inside, the muffled crump of its explosion, the door open again and the final burst of sub-machine gun fire to take care of any survivors.

'Shit on the Christmas tree!' Schulze cursed, as Lieutenant von Dodenburg ordered his platoon to prepare to go through the drill yet one more time, 'I don't think I'll ever be able to go through a door again without throwing an egg through it!' He wiped the sweat off his brow. 'If this goes on, I'm going to present a danger to society – real anti-social.'

Kuno von Dodenburg put on his helmet again and picked up his Schmeisser machine pistol. 'Schulze,' he said, 'you've been a danger to society ever since your old man conceived you. Come on, let's go!'

But Captain Geier was not prepared to follow the battalion commander's training schedule blindly. Privately he thought that Major Hartmann wouldn't survive the campaign to come. In spite of his name the Battalion Commander wasn't hard enough. For one thing he had a wife and children – always a bad sign in a professional soldier, in the Vulture's opinion. Besides Hartmann was too conventional; he did not expect the unexpected, like being faced with an opponent when one was not armed oneself.

Accordingly, after he had discovered to his delight that one of his NCOs had been in the pre-war police where he had learned the basic elements of ju-jitsu, the Vulture ordered that every man in the Second Company should learn the rudiments of unarmed combat. He was the first to undergo the course himself: a laughable little figure in his overlong shorts, dwarfed by the hulking ex-policeman. He found it very stimulating, apart from the basic stimulation of being close to another semi-nude sweating male body. But that was another and private matter, which was to be relegated to the back of his mind like the fading French postcards of naked boys were to the back of his dresser. 'Gentlemen,' he told his officers at their Monday morning conference with which he began each week, 'I want blind, fearless obedience. If I told you to jump out of that window, I would expect you to immediately, even though we are three floors up.' He screwed his monocle tighter into his right eye. 'And obedience is based on complete confidence in oneself. Hence I want my men to go through this course, every one of them. I can assure you that when they are finished, they will be afraid of no enemy in this world.'

'The weakest spot in a man's body,' the ex-policeman lectured them, 'is his balls. If you can get him there, he's had it. Get that?'

'Yes sergeant,' they replied in chorus.

'Now then, if you can get away with it with some Tommy or Frog, all right. But what are you going to do, if they try it on you?' He raised a big sausagelike finger in warning. 'That's the catch, isn't it?'

'Yes sergeant,' they chorused again obediently.

'However,' he continued, 'there is a defensive measure which I am going to reveal to you now. You Schulze, I want you to try to kick me in the balls.'

68

'Kick you in the balls Sergeant!' Schulze breathed in mock indignation. 'But you're an NCO!'

'Don't worry your poor little brain about that Schulze. I can take care of myself, believe you me. And don't be surprised if you're lying on your big fat arse in just a couple of seconds' time.'

'Are you sure, Sergeant?' Schulze asked.

'Of course, I'm sure. In fact, I'm ordering you to try and kick me in the balls.'

'Well, if that's the way it is, Sergeant, here we go.' Schulze streaked forward with surprising speed for such a big man. The NCO raised his hands to ward off the blow. Schulze sprang into the air. Like one of the pre-war stars of the Hamburg St Pauli football team he twisted in mid-air. The NCO was completely fooled. His hands grabbed and missed. The next instant he was lying crumpled on the floor, his chin covered in vomit, writhing from side to side.

'Do you think I should have told him I was the champion of the Barmbek Socialist Club's ju-jitsu team?' Schulze asked innocently.

And that was the end of the Vulture's attempts to turn his 2nd Company into expert unarmed combat fighters. But by now their CO had other things on his mind than the failure of his training programme. Time was running out, and the Company would have to carry out their assignment without the benefit of unarmed combat. On the evening of the last day of April, he ordered a company 'comrade evening'. He personally would provide two forty-eight litre casks of beer, while the other officers would purchase two dozen bottles of corn schnapps out of their own pockets.

The announcement, made by Sergeant-Major Metzger, was received with loud cheers from the men of the 2nd Company. But Schulze was not impressed. His elation at putting the ex-policeman out of action – the man was down-graded once he had recovered and transferred to some rear echelon unit – had vanished. His reaction to the announcement was a surly, 'Listen, when the gentlemen officers buy us commonfolk beer and schnapps, you can bet your last penny, the balloon's about to go up!'

And, as was usually the case, Schulze was not too far wrong...

CHAPTER SEVEN

Meine Herren!' Captain Geier rasped in his unmistakable Prussian voice, 'in a few moments we shall be going over to the men for the "comrade evening".' He tightened his grip on his monocle and stared at them – von Dodenburg, Schwarz, Kaufmann, whose father was a wealthy industrialist in the Ruhr, and young Fick, with his unfortunate name. 'I don't know your capacity for alcohol. All I expect from you is that you behave yourselves as gentlemen and officers.'

Schwarz looked at his CO with undisguised disgust. Underneath his cold cynical exterior, the Vulture was basically a bourgeois. Although he wore the uniform of the Führer's own Black Guards, he had no real understanding of the national revolution which had taken place under Adolf Hitler's leadership since 1933. In essence, Captain Geier was no better than the 'March Violets' who had flooded to join the National Socialist Party in the spring of that great year of German renewal, hoping to get on the bandwagon before it was too late.

The Vulture was no fool. He saw and understood Schwarz's look of contempt. 'You wait, my boy,' he promised Schwarz mentally, 'I'll have those breeches off you yet, Uncle Heydrich or no Uncle Heydrich!' But he was too wise a man to say the words. Instead he raised his glass of schnapps until it was level with the third button of his jacket, as military custom prescribed. Elbow at a ninety degree angle to his chest, he barked: *'Meine Herren – Prosit!'*

'*Prosit!*' they answered as one.

Like automatons, they raised their glasses, drank their drinks in one gulp and placed the empty glasses down on the table with a bang, all at exactly the same moment.

The Vulture nodded his appreciation. The uniformity of the movement pleased him, as did all uniformity. Admittedly they weren't cavalry officers and Schwarz and Kaufmann weren't gentlemen, but each one of them was a leader, a useful man in the battle soon to come. He cleared his throat. 'Gentlemen, I think it is time we went over to the men!'

Sergeant-Major Metzger had taken on the responsibility of decorating the room himself. The rough wooden tables were arranged in a great horseshoe and covered with grey blankets. At the head of the horseshoe there was a wooden armchair for the Vulture and ordinary chairs for his officers and the Sergeant-Major, with the normal dining-room benches extending to left and right for the men. At regular intervals there was a bottle of schnapps, surrounded by a cluster of little glasses; and before each individual seat there was a grey stone beer mug. Around the walls the men had nailed up pine branches stolen from the nearby state forest during the morning exercise. Now, as the Captain and his party entered, the men stood stiffly to attention behind their places. With pleasure the Vulture noted that a transformation had taken place in them in those few months. They seemed to have grown into their uniforms, which had long since lost their newness. Their faces were harder now and thinner, so that the eyes appeared to stand out more. They had learned a new code of conduct, where the concept of right and wrong was absolute and rigid; and they had learned it at the cost of cold, misery and, in some cases, at the cost of their own blood. Now they no longer looked like civilians masquerading as soldiers. They were trained soldiers, who lacked only one essential – the bloody experience of battle.

The Sergeant-Major gave the officers a magnificent salute. At the top of his voice, he bellowed. 'Second Company, SS Assault Battalion Wotan present for comrade evening, sir!'

The Vulture touched his gloved hand casually to his cap. 'Thank you, Sergeant-Major. Please stand the men at ease.'

There was an uneasy shuffling of feet. 'Break out the schnapps,' Metzger shouted officiously.

Hurriedly the glasses were passed round, the caps screwed off the bottles and the schnapps poured into them. The Vulture took off his big peaked cap and accepted a glass. He raised it rigidly to the third button of his tunic. 'Comrades,' he rasped, 'to us, the ones we love and the Second Company!'

'To us, the ones we love and the Second Company!' nearly two hundred voices bellowed so that the wooden beams rang to the sound.

'No heel taps!'

They finished their drink in one gulp, one or two of the younger ones, who had already filled their stomachs with olive oil and dry cheese for the ordeal, coughing as the *Korn* burned its way down their throats.

Geier sat down. The company followed with a noisy scraping back of the benches. 'Sergeant-Major,' he ordered, 'the company wit. A joke – a juicy one, please!'

'Schulze!' the Butcher yelled across the wooden table at the Hamburger.

'All right comedian, tell a joke – and you heard the Captain – a juicy one.'

Schulze did not hesitate. 'What did the soldier say to his wife after he had come home on leave for the first time in six months?'

'Well, what did he say?'

Schulze tugged at the end of his big nose. 'He said, "Take a good look at the floor, darling, because you're only going to be seeing the ceiling for the next forty-eight hours!"'

A wave of laughter ran down the table.

'Excellent, Schulze,' the Vulture said, pulling at his collar and accepting another schnapps. 'Now here's a really juicy one. Did you hear about the two warm brothers sailing

74

through the Kaiser-Wilhelm Canal...'
The comrade evening was under way.

The evening had degenerated into a noisy drunken confusion of voices, each trying to outbid the other in volume, letting off steam for the first time in months.

'Yer wrong,' they said, 'it's not that the Frogs is bad shots. It's because they aim at your balls. They're after making you into a singing tenor.'

'Well, with balls like yours, it'd be like aiming a 75mm cannon at a barn door!'

'Watch that shitty beer mug. You'll have it all over my uniform!'

'Once you've got your hand there, they can't resist anymore. Anybody knows that. The little man in the boat, that's the one you've got to tickle if you want them on their backs, ready and waiting for it.'

'So this feller shut him up right smartish. Right in front of everybody he got up and said at the top of his voice, "You've got to excuse my friend. He's just had an unfortunate love affair." Of course everybody was waiting to know what the love affair was. And so he said, "Yes, he broke the wrist of his right hand last week!" Jesus Christ, you should have heard the silence!'

'This recruit pulled out the nail and said to the kitchen bull, "Look sergeant, a nail!" and the kitchen bull asked, "What kinda nail –

human or the one you knock in wood?" "The kind you knock in wood!" So the kitchen bull said, all cool, calm and collected, "Get it down you, soldier, it'll put iron in yer!"'

So the evening progressed: an endless, confused parade of old jokes, beer, traditional soldiers' lore, beer, complaints, beer, snatches of dirty songs, beer, all punctuated by sudden dashes to the latrines to get rid of the excess liquid.

'Let me tell you, Lieutenant Schwarz,' the Butcher said drunkenly, towering over the little officer, a beer mug in one hand a glass of schnapps in the other, 'I can even smell a Yid!' He waved one hand, as if to ward off a protest and spilled some of his beer on Schwarz's gleaming boots. The officer did not even notice.

'Everybody knows they smell different to us. That's why the MO sticks his nose in your armpit during the medical.' He nodded his big head significantly. 'You see they've been trained at university to recognise a Yid's smell at once. But me, I don't need training. I grew up with them.' He glowered suddenly. 'Big-nosed bastards with plenty of money. A smart, greasy lot, always after the girls – our girls. They like white meat, you know.'

'Is that so?' Schwarz said drunkenly, finding it difficult not to slur the three simple words, and deciding it would be better, if he tried them again. *'Is that so?'*

'Naturally, Lieutenant,' the Butcher said significantly and took another deep drink of his beer, following it with a chaser of schnapps. 'They'd do anything for white meat. Our blonde German girls fas-fascinate them, you see. But they never marry them. Couldn't even then, even before our Führer came to power. Where I used to live as a lad, they used to say that the Rabbi would threaten to dock it off altogether with his knife if they said they wanted to marry a German girl.'

Schwarz's mouth dropped open incredulously. 'Is that so?' he breathed.

The Butcher leered at him. 'It is Lieutenant. As if them Yiddish tails hadn't been chopped short enough as it is, eh!'

'Look here, Schulze,' von Dodenburg said a little angrily, 'an army can only function efficiently when an order is carried out unconditionally.'

'Even a stupid order?' the other asked with the dogged persistence of the drunk. 'A stupid one, Lieutenant?'

'There are no stupid orders, Schulze. They may appear stupid to you soldiers. But you are the recipients and you can't really judge, can you?'

'But what about that captain in the 1st

Company who ordered his driver to jump out of the window – and the silly arsehole did and broke his leg?' Schulz persisted. 'What did that prove, sir?'

'It proved that the soldier in question had absolute confidence in his officer.'

'Well, I don't look at it like that, sir,' Schulze said. 'It seems to me that it ain't any different to the old cadaver obedience of the Kaiser's day that my Dad used to tell me about.' He took a deep drink of his beer.

Eagerly von Dodenburg seized on the expression. 'Cadaver obedience! No, you're completely wrong there, Schulze. There's nothing like it in our training. The leadership of the SS wouldn't tolerate it. General Berger's theories are absolutely to the contrary.' Full of drunken enthusiasm he began to lecture Schulze on the 'Duke of Swabia's' principles of military training.

Standing in the middle of the noisy room, stroking his big nose and looking, with his completely bald head, more like a vulture than ever, Captain Geier felt happy, or as happy as he could ever feel. Around him were the young men of his company, their faces were still unlined by the marks of corruption, unlike those of the painted youngsters he was forced to have recourse to in Berlin.

These young men looked good. For a moment he allowed himself to muse on what they must look like naked – hard, muscular young bodies, unlike the soft effete bodies of the young men cruising the dark streets behind Berlin's Lehrter Station. Then he dismissed the thought as unworthy.

'Duty is duty,' he told himself, using the old service phrase, 'and schnapps is schnapps. And the two should not be mixed.' The beautiful boys were part of another world and nothing to do with his military existence.

A 'beer corpse' passed, borne by six giggling, drunken soldiers. They had placed the drunk on one of the benches and were bearing him towards the latrines. 'We're going to give him a state funeral, sir,' one of the bearers told the Captain excitedly. The Vulture smiled thinly and touched his hand to his forehead in salute, as was expected from him. The procession passed on, a drunken parody of the real thing.

The Vulture took one last look at his company. *'My company,'* he whispered softly to himself and felt tears come to his eyes, as he wondered how many of these handsome young men, the élite of the nation, would survive what was to come.

He pulled himself together and pushed his way through the crowd. 'Sergeant-Major,' he snapped in his customary nasal voice.

The Butcher, his face as red as beetroot, his eyes gleaming with drink, swung round drunkenly and, swaying badly, tried to assume the position of attention.

Captain Geier waved to him to desist. 'Not here, Sergeant-Major,' he said. 'I just wanted to tell you that the officers are leaving now. It is better that we leave the men to get on with it.' He took one last look around him, as if he were trying to register their faces for some private roll of honour. 'Goodnight, Sergeant-Major,' he said and touched his hand to his cap before striding out, followed by his officers, who trotted after him like drunken puppies.

The victims continued their celebration.

He had picked her up under the thin blue light of the blacked-out street lamp after following the tap-tap of the high-heeled shoes on the wet cobbles with drunken persistence. As he had been unable to see her face on the way to her apartment, his attention had been concentrated on running his hands up and down her body under the gleaming black mac.

But now he saw that she was beautiful, her eyes a deep black under the short curly hair, her face a smooth sweet oval. He could almost believe that she was unspoiled and innocent.

But she wasn't. The cunning expert kisses she gave him told even his drunken brain that.

Yet he was too drunk and too eager to care

any longer. His hands followed the seam of her silk stocking, searching for the white skin above, smooth, firm and utterly enchanting.

Violently he pushed her on her back. Automatically her legs flew open. He caught a glimpse of that dark hairy flower, set deep in its wet V. He bored his hard body into hers, and suddenly he had forgotten the world of men, with its jackboots, crisp orders, steel monsters, and its smell of impending death.

As he slept exhausted, his blond hair matted damply to his forehead, the unknown woman stroked the back of his neck with infinite compassion.

Schwarz wandered blindly through the blacked-out town. A fat middle-aged policeman spotted him as he staggered into the blue light cast by the street lamp. Officiously he clapped his hand on his duty pistol, but when he saw the officer's stars and the silver gleam of the SS runes he turned and strode hurriedly away in the other direction.

Schwarz staggered on. The town was blacked-out perfectly. But behind every shuttered window he seemed to sense music, happy voices, laughter. They made him feel sad – that heartbreaking maudlin sadness of the drunk, whom no one loves in the whole wide world. Schwarz felt empty. He had no friends, no comrades even, only superiors and subordinates. No girl to love him – not even one of the cheap whores that the men lined up to visit in the house behind the barracks. He was completely, utterly, irrevocably alone in this world.

Suddenly he found himself looking up at a tall un-German building that had the appearance of a church, but wasn't one. Its boarded-up door and broken windows, which had not been opened these two years or more stared back at him blankly. His unsteady gaze fell on the swastika painted on the door and the bold red letters 'Jews Out!' Then he realised, with a feeling of disgust and fascination, that he was standing in front of the local synagogue, which had obviously suffered the fate of all German Jewish churches during the 'Crystal Night' of 1938.

On impulse he staggered up the steps, still littered with glass from that terrible night when the Trier SA had come in their official cars, had pulled off the Rabbi's Iron Cross from the First War, which he had thought would protect him from their anger, and strung him up in the square. It had taken him twenty minutes to die. His shoulder pushed against the door which gave immediately, as it had done that November night when the jack-booted SA troopers had come in yelling at the tops of their voices to plunder the place of worship, urinating in the sacred places, destroying what they could not take with them, egged on by the screams of the crowd outside.

Schwarz stood swaying in the interior, illuminated only by the light of the stars which shone through the hole in the roof.

He searched the littered floor for a stone and flung it at the nearest wall. It clattered to the ground somewhere in the shadows. 'I'm not a Jew,' he screamed. 'Do you hear? *I'm not a Jew.*' His cry against the dirty trick that fate had played on him was swallowed up in the furthest recesses of the bat-infested roof. 'Jew,' it mocked him. 'Jew, Jew, Jew, Jew.' He clapped his hands over his ears and tried to block out the accusing word.

In the seclusion of his bedroom, behind a locked door, Captain Geier leafed through his well-worn collection of photos, staring at the young male bodies, while the ancient upright clock which he had inherited from his father ticked away the minutes of his life.

CHAPTER EIGHT

'Gentlemen, we march! In ten days at the latest, seven at the earliest!'

The Vulture sat back on the mounted cavalry saddle which served him as an office chair and stared at their earnest faces with pleasure. The announcement had had the expected effect.

'Where to, sir?' von Dodenburg asked.

'I am afraid that I cannot tell you that – on express orders from the Battalion CO who was at Army Group with the rest of the battalion commanders this morning. The Führer, in his wisdom, has decreed that individual targets will not be told to those assigned to them until the very last moment. My guess is that I shall be able to tell you in a couple of days' time.'

'But sir,' von Dodenburg protested. 'We've got to know something. General Berger says...'

'I know what General Berger says,' the Vulture interrupted him. 'We of the *old* Officers Corps,' he emphasised the word 'old', 'know only too well what his opinions are. However, if I cannot give you any details about your immediate assignment, I *can* sketch in the general situation, as explained by the battalion commander.'

Striding over to the big map of Western Europe on the wall, he tapped it with his riding cane. 'The Western Front. For over seven months now, over a million men have been facing each other on a front of five hundred kilometres from the Swiss border to the so-called English Channel, with hardly a shot being fired for all that time. Last year when we invaded Poland, the Anglo-French forces missed their opportunity of hitting us while your West Wall was denuded of our best troops. Now it is time that the forces of Greater Germany show the enemy how to conduct a campaign. But where?'

Thoughtfully he tapped the map with his cane. 'Here in Alsace in the Belfort Gap, a classic invasion route, which I am sure you are all familiar with – even those of you who slept through the military history classes at Bad Toelz. But the Belfort Gap is covered by the French Maginot Line. As is the Lorraine Gap around Metz-Verdun.' He tapped the map a little higher up. 'But it too is protected by some of France's most effective and powerful fortifications. So what is left to us?'

Von Dodenburg nodded to the shaded area of neutral Belgium. 'The Losheim Gap between Aachen and Prum.'

The Vulture beamed appreciatively. 'I see *you* didn't sleep through the military history lectures, von Dodenburg,' he said. 'Of course; the third of the classic invasion routes into France's northern plain. But, naturally, it has one great disadvantage.'

Schwarz clicked his heels together, as if he were an officer cadet again and barked. 'Highly unsuitable country for modern warfare, sir. The road system is inadequate for a modern motorised army and the terrain is wooded and most suitable for armoured formations, which undoubtedly will be the spearhead of any German force attacking westwards.'

The Vulture nodded his approval. 'Highly commendable, Schwarz. We will make a general staff officer of you yet. Your words reflect the opinion of the German General Staff – almost to the man.' He hesitated and von Dodenburg thought he saw the faint shadow of a cynical smile cross his CO's ugly, birdlike face. 'In his wisdom, the Führer has decided, however, that this will be the area in which the bulk of our forces will attack.'

'In the Ardennes, sir?' they asked, almost as one. 'But that's impossible.'

He held up his cane for silence and screwed his monocle more firmly in his eye. 'Gentlemen, I am surprised at you! Nothing is impossible for the Führer.' Again von Dodenburg sensed the CO's underlying cynicism. 'You, as National Socialist officers, should know that, even more than an unpolitical chap like myself, who has never voted in an election in his whole life. And God forbid that I will ever have to either.' He paused. 'Anyway let me explain our plan.'

He tapped the Low Countries on the big map. 'The obvious method of avoiding the French Maginot Line would be to sweep through Belgium as we did in 1914. But it is so obvious that the British and French general staffs, who are not noted for their intelligence or insight, plan to oppose such an opening gambit by moving the bulk of the Anglo-French forces into Belgium.'

'In other words, the enemy expects us to come through Belgium. The question that the Führer must have asked himself is, "Where does he expect us to attack?"' He tapped the Ardennes area with his cane. 'Definitely not here. As a result it is the Führer's intention to make a feint with his right wing so that the enemy will start rushing into Belgium. As soon as that movement is underway, the bulk of our armoured forces will strike through the Ardennes. The tankers will crack through the French here at Sedan.' He indicated the legendary city on the Franco-Belgian border, which had seen the greatest triumph of Prussian arms in the Franco-Prussian War and had led to the creation of the German national state. 'With Sedan taken, our armour will head west along the north bank of the Somme for the Channel.' He hesitated momentarily and when he spoke again all the cynicism had vanished from his voice to be replaced by scarcely concealed tension and excitement. 'And, gentlemen, if we can bring that movement off, it will be the end of the Anglo-French armies and the greatest victory of German arms ever. Perhaps even the greatest victory that any one nation has ever won.'

The next forty-eight hours were given over to careful last-minute preparations for the battle to come. It seemed as if Assault Battalion Wotan held a different parade every second hour to check some piece of equipment or other, from paybooks to ascertain if every soldier had received the requisite number of injections for field service, to a major all-night inspection of the halftracks which would carry them into battle.

In the midst of this anxious preparation for sudden death, there were some who had other more personal business to occupy them – Sergeant-Major Metzger, for instance.

Three days after the 'comrade evening', the Butcher had felt a painful burning sensation when he urinated in the morning. It was as if a hot rod were being thrust slowly up his penis. Then the pain passed away and in the hectic atmosphere of the company office, he forgot about it, until three hours later when he had drunk his 11 o'clock 'half litre' and had made his way to the NCOs' latrine to enjoy his usual long sit over the *Volkischer Beobachter*. But this particularly morning, there was no pleasure to be had for Sergeant-Major Metzger. He had hardly let down his immaculate field-grey trousers and begun to urinate when he was forced to hold on to the wall in excruciating pain, the sweat standing out in great opaque beads on his crimson face, the liquid squirting out of him in five different directions.

The Butcher had been in the Army long enough to know what he had got. But where? Not from Fat Barbara, the whore he usually frequented in the establishment behind the barracks; he hadn't been to her place for three months now. In fact, he hadn't been with any woman except his wife in that period. And he didn't believe it was possible to get the disease from a latrine seat as some of the older NCOs still persisted in believing.

Lore then? That was impossible! Something must have happened on the night the Company got drunk. But what? He had a vague memory of talking to Lieutenant Schwarz about the Yids, but after that his mind was completely blank.

That midday he didn't go home, although he knew that Lore had cooked his favourite meal of sauerkraut and pig's knuckle. The senior NCOs of the other companies, who preferred to take their dinner in liquid form in the wet canteen, made pointed remarks about his saving it up till Lore had 'warmed up supper' for him in front of the oven. But he ignored them; he was too preoccupied with his attempts to discover what he had done on the night of the company drinking session. Nobody seemed to know.

Puzzled, he returned to the company office. But he could not sit still. Every five minutes he would rise to go to the NCOs latrine, where he would slip down his pants and examine his penis. Now a thin yellowish pus oozed out of it when he squeezed it.

In the office, the two clerks winked at each other knowingly every time he disappeared. 'The Butcher's got the shits,' they whispered to each other. 'He knows we're going on active service. I bet the bastard's going to spin that cracked pill-roller some sort of tale so that he can get out of going with us.'

And to some extent the movement order, which the Butcher knew now rested in the company safe, did play a part in his calculations. If he did report sick, he knew that he would not have to go into action with the Battalion – and the Butcher was very much concerned with the safety of his own hide. But if he did report sick, he knew that the Vulture would ensure that that would be the end of his military career. A suspicious bastard like the Vulture would immediately suspect he had infected himself to get out of the dangers which lay before them. Before the day would be out, he would be reduced to the ranks, transferred to a military prison hospital and from there eventually to one of the dreaded punishment battalions.

In the end, the Butcher decided to go to a

doctor, but not to the Battalion MO with his idiotic nature curses. Instead, he borrowed the company cycle and pedalled into the little garrison town to visit the local doctor, *Dr Med* Hans Friderichs.

The aged local doctor, who like the one hundred per cent catholic population of the town, had little time for the SS, although he had twice voted for Adolf Hitler in the thirties, listened to the Sergeant-Major's stumbling explanation, then snapped, 'Trousers down, and hold on to that table – firmly.'

'Why?' the Butcher asked a little fearfully, as he fumbled with his braces.

The bespectacled little doctor who, as a young military doctor in Stenay in the First World War had dealt with two or three hundred VD cases a day, mumbled, 'You'll soon find out.'

He pulled a rubber stool over his forefinger and stuck it up the Butcher's anus.

The Sergeant-Major yelped with pain. 'What did you do that for?' he grumbled. 'The trouble's at the other end, doctor. Not in my arse.'

'Keep still,' the doctor ordered and began to work his finger in more deeply.

Five minutes later, the doctor leaned over the microscope in the corner, staring at the sample he had obtained, the Butcher hung numbly on the edge of the table, his head bent, as if in defeat. The doctor took off his gold-rimmed spectacles and looked grimly at the NCO, his faded eyes full of *schadenfreude*. 'I am afraid, my dear Sergeant-Major, that you have caught gonorrhoea, as far as I can ascertain from a quick examination.'

'But that's impossible,' the Butcher exclaimed. 'I haven't been with a woman for months except my–' he broke off suddenly, overwhelmed by the tremendous magnitude of that abrupt realization. The doctor shrugged. 'My dear man, I hope that, as a member of the Black Guards,' he could not resist the sneer, 'the representative of a newer and better Germany, you do not believe that one can contract the disease without sexual intercourse!'

The Butcher did not reply. When he was cured, he promised himself, he'd punch the bastard in his sneering face. But that would have to come later; first he must be cured. 'No doctor,' he answered hesitantly. 'No, of course not.'

'Good. Now get yourself onto the couch in the corner and stretch out on your back.'

With his trousers around his ankles, he struggled over to the couch looking absurdly like a small child who had wet his pants. He stretched himself out on the cold leather of the couch. The little doctor bent over him and with his thumb and forefinger, he lifted up Butcher's penis as if it were exceedingly filthy and slipped a small dressing round it.

With difficulty the Butcher craned his head and said, 'What are you going to do, doctor?'

The doctor turned to his tray of instruments. 'In France, the soldiers used to call it the umbrella,' he said with a faint smile at the memory. It was the first time he had used the soldiers' term in nearly a quarter of a century.

'The umbrella?' the Butcher asked, a horrid realization beginning to dawn on him.

'Yes – a special catheter we use in this kind of business,' he explained. He raised the instrument so that the Butcher could see it and pressed the little catch at its base. A series of small blades sprang out at the other end. The Butcher swallowed hard. In spite of the coldness of the leather, he felt the sweat start up all down his back.

'That,' he gulped, 'in there?'

'Yes, in there!'

As the doctor seized his penis firmly and inserted the catheter, a look of pleasure on his ancient wrinkled face, the Butcher screamed in agony.

Sergeant-Major Metzger was limping badly when he emerged from the surgery. After the treatment, the doctor had told him he could go and urinate. But when he saw the blood shoot out of his maltreated organ, he stopped immediately. Now his bladder felt as if it were about to burst. But he bit his lip and resisted the urge. In fact, he was just swearing to himself that he would probably never urinate again, when he almost bumped into Private Schulze. 'Schulze,' he exclaimed in surprise, and regretted the next moment that he had raised his voice, 'what the devil are you doing here, man?'

Schulze, standing rigidly to attention, said, 'Going to see the doctor, Sergeant-Major.'

'Why don't you go to the MO?' Metzger asked.

'Marital problem, sir,' Schulze replied. 'Didn't think the MO would be the right man for it.'

'Oh,' the Butcher said without much interest. 'I didn't even know you were married.' Then, in a voice that was almost human, he added, 'But I know what you mean. Wives are good for nothing but trouble!'

He acknowledged Schulze's salute carefully and left him.

'You're right there, mate,' Schulze sighed and grinned in spite of the pain. 'Poor old Lore'll be in for the worst hiding of her life as soon as the Butcher gets home,' he thought to himself. He opened the door and steeled himself to face the music.

Twelve hours later the Battalion was ready to move, the long column of heavily-laden halftracks parked around the barrack square under the trees, hidden from the curious gaze of British and French reconnaissance planes. On their wooden bunks the young men, exhausted yet too excited to sleep, waited for the call which must soon come.

CHAPTER NINE

'Gentlemen,' the Vulture said, hardly able to contain his own excitement, 'we have our orders at last! And they are better than I could possibly have expected. There'll be a piece of tin in this for all of you, believe you me!'

The Vulture strode over to the big trestle table and pulled back the grey army blanket which covered the model. 'Eben-Emael,' he announced triumphantly, 'the most impregnable fortification in Europe, stronger than anything we have in our own West Wall and naturally better than the Maginot Line!'

The officers crowded closer to examine the detailed model of Belgium's key fortified area, which guarded the junction of the River Meuse and the Albert Canal and barred the way to the plain of Northern France.

'According to Admiral Canaris' men,' Captain Geier lectured them as if they were

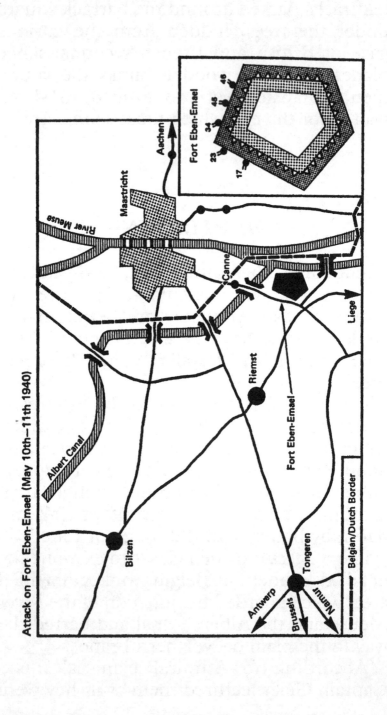

Attack on Fort Eben-Emael (May 10th–11th 1940)

back at Bad Toelz, 'Fort Eben-Emael is con-
structed in a series of concrete and steel
underground galleries. How deep, the
Abwehr agents do not know. However, we do
know that the gun turrets are protected by
the thickest armour that Liege can provide
and are expected to be able to withstand the
heaviest known bomb or artillery shell.' He
chuckled softly. 'But the Belgians are not
aware that we have a secret weapon to take
care of that armour – our hollow charges.
That, however, is the problem of the
engineers.'

'And our problem, sir?' von Dodenburg
said softly, eyeing the model of the Belgian
fortification, which he knew had been
thoroughly modernized in 1935 and was
expected to hold up any enemy for an
indefinite period.

'General Student's airborne division had
been training a special force of parachute engineers for the last six months for the task of
making the initial attack on Eben-Emael,' the
Vulture explained. 'Eighty men or so under
the command of a certain Captain Witzig.'

'*Eighty men!*' they said incredulously '*To
take that place?* The garrison alone must
number several hundreds.'

'One thousand, two hundred to be exact,'
the Vulture said calmly. 'With elements of
the Belgian 7th infantry Division, the
Cyclistes Frontière, and perhaps the best

troops the Belgians have at the frontier, the *Chasseurs Ardennais,* in the immediate area of the fortifications.' He glanced around their earnest young faces. 'But, gentlemen, I am surprised at you that you should doubt German ingenuity for one single moment! Apart from our hollow charges, we have another surprise up our sleeves. Captain Witzig is going to land with his men by glider – *on top of Fort Eben-Emael!*'

The Captain could not conceal his satisfaction at the look of surprise which sprang to their faces. 'It will be their task to keep the garrison occupied, while we advance towards them, link up and reduce the fort.' He said the words without any emphasis, as if he were talking about a normal route march, an everyday routine exercise; yet a quick glance at the model on the table sufficed to tell them that the link-up would be anything but a walkover. The River Meuse would have to be crossed and the Albert Canal, plus what looked like a medieval moat, even before they could come within striking distance of the great fort's bristling guns.

'Our line of march will take us from Maastricht,' the Vulture went on, tapping the model with his cane to emphasize each point he made, 'over the Meuse by one of the three bridges. The village of Canne – here – will be taken by Company One by storm. We will jump over them and cross the Albert Canal

98

here. Thereafter the Third Company was scheduled to take over from us and attack the key gun emplacements – 17, 23, 36, 45 and 46. As you can see from the model, they cover the whole length of the river and the canal. As long as they are in Belgian hands, a mass crossing of our armies is impossible. In essence they are the key to the door of Belgium and Northern France.'

He looked at them solemnly, without a trace of the usual cynicism in his face. 'However, I asked the commander if this company could have the honour of taking those emplacements. I hope you will agree that I acted in your best interests.'

The officers clicked to attention. Von Dodenburg spoke for the rest. 'As the company officer, sir, we are indebted to you for your foresight. It will be a great honour for the company, which will be appreciated by the men, I am sure.'

'Thank you, von Dodenburg. I am certain you are right. Undoubtedly the men will be duly appreciative when they learn the honour which has been granted them. The Battalion Commander thought it might be too much for the 2nd Company, but I assured him that we could do it. Now I must rely upon you and the men to ensure that I am not proved a liar.' He grinned. 'After all, gentlemen, as I am sure you are all well aware, I want to come out of this campaign with my major's insignia.'

There was no answering smile on their serious young faces. 'Boors,' Geier thought contemptuously, 'ideological boors!' But he kept the thought to himself. He would need them in the days to come and, when they were dead, other eager young ideological fools, avid for a violent death in the cause of 'Folk, Fatherland and Führer', if he were to realise his dream of becoming a general officer.

Stretching himself to his full height, he said, 'Gentlemen, you realise the importance of our task. If we fail, we hold up the whole advance of the Wehrmacht. In essence, the success of the whole campaign lies in our hands. And we have exactly thirty-six hours to complete our assignment.' His eyes flashed round their faces. *'Meine Herren, Heil Hitler!'*

They responded with all the fervour of their youthful hearts, typical products of the National Socialist dream, with its loud effrontery, brown-shirted vulgarity and jack-booted cruelty and which would soon demand its sacrifice in blood from them.

Shortly before midnight on 9 May, 1940, the halftracks rattled through the gate of the Adolf Hitler Barracks for the last time. The blacked-out cobbled streets of the town were empty, and as the metallic noise of their vehicles reverberated between the houses, no one opened his shutters to stare. Instead the simple Catholic peasants hurried to kneel in front of the plain wooden crucifixes which were the sole decoration in most of the bedrooms.

The Black Guards – SS Assault Battalion Wotan – were going to war.

SECTION TWO:
BAPTISM OF FIRE

'What terrible scruples you have for an SS officer! Don't you realise that a whole army is lining up behind us and behind that a whole nation of eighty million souls? In the face of that, what is important or even significant about the lives of a few obscure civilians?' *Captain Geier to Kuno v. Dodenburg, 11 May, 1940*

CHAPTER ONE

Moonlight flooded the cobbled frontier road. Up ahead a faint pink glow tinged the clouds. On both sides the torn-up fields were filled with the long shadows of the waiting Mark IVs, and the halftracks carrying the men of Assault Battalion Wotan.

Somewhere a slow, old-fashioned Dutch machine gun was chattering like an angry woodpecker and white and red tracer zigzagged through the night. But the enemy fire and the prospect of violent action soon to come did not worry the SS men any longer. They had been waiting outside the Dutch city of Maastricht for over two hours now and they were bored. It seemed an age since the great black shapes of the DFS 230 gliders, carrying the paras, had slid over their heads on their way to Fort Eben-Emael, towed by the three-engined Junkers. 'Hurry up and wait,' they complained softly as they smoked, hands carefully cupped around the glowing ends of their cigarettes, 'the same old Army game.'

'Don't the Dutch know there's a war on?' Schulze snorted to von Dodenburg as they sat together in his Volkswagen jeep, waiting for the order to move. 'If this is total war, give me…' He was interrupted by the noise of a motorbike roaring up the road towards them, weaving its way in and out of the traffic. Its rider recognized the halftracks and braked hard. The mud-splattered bike skidded sideways towards them for a good five yards. The rider sprang from the saddle and let the bike spin into a ditch.

It was the Vulture, his uniform covered in mud, a blood-stained bandage wrapped round his head, his monocle still clamped in his eye.

Von Dodenburg sprang out of the Volkswagen in alarm. 'What happened, sir?'

'Nothing, nothing!' he panted. 'That damnfool driver of mine went over one of our own mines. Now he's dead and I hit my head on a stanchion.' He waved his hand irritably. 'But that's of no matter! The paras have landed on the Eben-Emael plateau, though not in the numbers expected. Witzig, their commander, is missing.' He paused to catch his breath. 'Heavy fighting!' From the south-west came the thump of a heavy gun, followed by a spurt of flame, as if to emphasize his words.

'All very confused at the moment, as usual. One thing is certain. The paras haven't taken their objective at Canne.'

'The bridge, sir?' von Dodenburg asked.

'No, the enemy blew it up before they

could rush it.' Geier shook his bandaged head. 'A bad blow for us. It'll hold us up. But that's of no matter. The Battalion Commander has ordered me to push on immediately with the Second Company.'

Von Dodenburg pointed to the blocked road ahead. 'Impossible, sir,' he said, raising his voice as the firing on the other side of the border began to increase in intensity. 'We'll never be able to get through that mess with our halftracks.'

'You think so? Tell your men to mount up and I'll show you how it's done!'

While the halftracks roared into life the Vulture doubled over to the nearest Mark IV. 'You!' he barked to the black-uniformed tanker smoking on its turret, 'What's your rank?'

'Sergeant, sir!'

'And your unit?'

'The Fourth Panzer.'

'Good, well now you're attached to the SS.'

'But sir,' the sergeant protested.

'No buts!' Geier cried above the roar, clambering up on the turret, 'head right into that column up there and clear a path for my men!'

The NCO hesitated, then he caught a glimpse of the SS officer's face and changed his mind. Hurriedly he clambered into his turret and began to rap out orders. The tank's diesels whined. A throaty cough, followed a second later by the ear-splitting roar of the 230 HP engine. The night air was heavy with the stink of diesel oil.

The Vulture waved his blue torch at the halftracks. Von Dodenburg jerked his elbow into Schulze's ribs. 'All right,' he yelled, 'you saw the signal. Move after him!'

Schulze rammed home first gear. 'This I've got to see,' he cried, as the halftracks began to clatter onto the road.

The Mark IV moved forward with a rusty chattering of tracks. Hurriedly the waiting *Wehrmacht* infantry sprang out of the way. Angry cries went up on all sides. 'What's going on?' an officer shouted. 'What the devil do you think you're about?' Then he caught a momentary glimpse of the silver SS runes. 'Ah, ah!' he shouted bitterly, 'the gentlemen from the SS! So that's it!'

Geier, towering up above him on the tank turret, waved his cane. 'Yes, the gentlemen from the SS going to war!'

They rolled on. On both sides of the road the pitiful procession of the walking wounded began to make their appearance, toiling back to the regimental aid posts. Suddenly a train of horse-drawn artillery loomed up in front of the tank. The driver took his foot off the accelerator instinctively. The Vulture slashed at the tank sergeant with his cane. *'Don't stop!'* he cried in a frenzy of rage. *'Tell him to keep on going!'*

Holding his smarting face with his right hand, the sergeant kicked the driver's shoulder to indicate he should increase his speed again. The Mark IV smashed right into the unsuspecting column. Horses plunged and whinnied in panic. Drivers cursed as their carts swung precariously close to the ditches on both sides of the road. Angry shouts rose on all sides, as the halftracks rattled on behind the tanks, with the SS men jeering: 'Make way for the Wotan Battalion, you damned stubble-hoppers, you!'

Just as the pre-dawn sky began to break up into the dirty white which heralded the morning, the Vulture directed the Mark IV off the cobbled road onto a rough track. Now they were getting very close to the scene of the fighting. Above the line of dark firs, which marched across the horizon like a column of spike-helmeted Prussian grenadiers, there were constant soft puffs of grey smoke. Both sides of the track were littered with abandoned equipment, German and Belgian. Next to a pillbox, which the shellfire of the initial barrage had pocked as if with the symptoms of some disease, a German tank was burning fiercely.

Schulze cursed as he manoeuvred the Volkswagen round a dead body sprawled in the middle of the road. 'This is like a

Strength through Joy tour,' he said. 'Germany, Holland, and now Belgium.'

'Shut up, Schulze!' von Dodenburg snapped, concentrating on the tank in front of them, 'and watch you don't land us in the ditch!'

As Schulze changed up again and increased speed, he guessed that Geier had guided the company around Maastricht and its clogged-up narrow streets. Now they must be getting close to the Belgian frontier and the first water barrier, the River Meuse. The dead Belgian soldier and the abandoned equipment proved that.

Warily he eyed the dark pine woods on both sides. Behind him the young troopers in the halftracks took up their positions, gripping their weapons tensely; this was an ideal place for ambush, as the burning tank indicated.

But nothing happened. The woods gave way to open fields, which still glistened with the early morning dew. In front of them a small hamlet loomed up. Nothing stirred. Not even a dog barked.

Geier thumped the sergeant on the shoulder. 'Tell the driver to move round to the left of the houses,' he ordered. 'My men will cover you.'

'But sir,' the sergeant protested, his mind still full of the charred body of the dead tanker sprawled out in the road behind them, 'that village is an obvious place for an ambush. I don't like it. I think...'

'You're not paid to think, sergeant,' Geier interrupted him.

As the Mark IV stopped momentarily while the sergeant gave his driver the order, Geier dropped over the side and doubled back to von Dodenburg's Volkswagen. 'Quick,' he yelled, 'get your vehicles off the track!'

While the tank rumbled forward like an awkward metal duck waddling towards a pond, the halftracks clattered into the fields on both sides of the track. Schulze and von Dodenburg stood upright behind the windscreen to watch it as it got closer and closer to the silent village, its 75mm cannon swinging from side to side like the snout of some predatory monster seeking its prey.

Schulze thrust back his helmet and wiped the sweat off his face. 'All this tension is no good for my nerves, sir. I think I'll apply for a posting back to Hamburg as soon as the company office comes...'

He stopped in mid-sentence, interrupted by a violent explosion from the direction of the village. The first shell shattered the stillness of the morning.

'Holy shit!' von Dodenburg cursed. 'An anti-tank cannon!'

His words were drowned by the echoing boom of metal striking metal. The Mark IV lurched to a halt. For a moment nothing seemed to happen. Then a great orange-yellow flame leaped into the air. Schulze ducked hurriedly as huge metal splinters, glowing red-hot, hissed towards them. He caught a last glimpse of the tankers, screaming frantically as their black uniforms began to crackle with flames, clutching the turret with charred fingers in their attempt to escape; then the windscreen shattered and he could see no more.

'Just as I thought,' Geier said as they crouched in the ditch, listening to the whine of the ricochets and the ragged chatter of the enemy machine guns.

Von Dodenburg looked at his CO incredulously. 'You mean, you knew the village was held? You sacrificed the tank?'

Geier shrugged. 'What's one tank? A couple of fools who joined the Tank Corps because they thought it was easier and safer than the infantry. Now they've learned their lesson.' He grinned. 'Unfortunately, a little too late.' He changed the subject. 'According to my map, the Meuse is on the other side of that village. Probably over the rise. If we can get through that rabble holding the village, we'll reach it hours ahead of the rest of the battalion.'

Kuno did not think it opportune to point out that the 'rabble' in the buildings around the church were doing a damn good job of holding up a company of Black Guards. Instead he listened attentively while Geier explained his plan:

'A pincer-movement in other words. You take the left column of halftracks, I'll take the right. Smash right into them with all you've got! And remember – don't worry about casualties! We *must* get through to the river. Do you understand?'

In that instant Kuno realised that the Vulture would sacrifice the life of every man in the company to achieve his aim. The CO's dark eyes were empty of any emotion, completely empty. The next moment he was making a mad dash for the halftracks, hidden by the dead ground to the rear, enemy bullets stitching a vicious trail at his heels.

The first halftrack was hit and came to an abrupt halt. Behind it the broken track lay flopped out like a severed limb. Another was hit in the gasoline tank. It went up in flames immediately, its exploding ammunition zig-zagging into the sky at crazy angles. The troopers bailed out frantically, leaving the dead and dying in their burning coffins.

A grenade sailed through the air and landed to the rear of von Dodenburg's crowded halftrack. *'Duck, sir,'* Schulze yelled. It exploded with a sharp vicious crack and shrapnel hissed through the air. Next to von

Dodenburg, the driver cursed and clapped a hand to his shoulder. Blood started to spurt through his tightly clutched-together fingers, his head dropped to the wheel and before Schulze could grab it, the halftrack lurched into a ditch where its axle broke with a sudden crash.

'Bail out!' von Dodenburg yelled.

The survivors needed no urging. While von Dodenburg grabbed the heavy machine gun mounted on the cab and sprayed the houses to their front, they levered themselves over the metal sides, pressing their bodies close to the armour to present the smallest target possible.

'Don't leave me!' someone screamed from the bottom of the halftrack. A badly wounded man, his hands held close to his shattered stomach, staggered to his feet and tried to clamber over the side. As he did so, he moved his hands. His whole stomach was ripped open and he fell forward over the side of the half-track, dead.

Schulze suddenly felt all energy drain out of him. The dead man was the boy he had helped over the wall of the assault course. Now, within ten minutes of going into action, he was dead. It had all been for nothing.

'Schulze, for God's sake, get out of here – before the bastard goes up!' von Dodenburg yelled and pushed him out of the shattered cab. Thick white smoke, tinged with oil, was beginning to pour from the engine.

'Follow me!' von Dodenburg cried above the roar, placing his hand, fingers outspread, on the crown of his helmet – the infantry sign for 'rally on me'. Without waiting to check if they were doing so, he rushed forward, firing his machine pistol from the hip as he ran. In a ragged bunch, his men followed.

A soldier in a coal-scuttle helmet, his face contorted with fear, leaped up from behind a manure heap. In his hand he held a grenade.

Von Dodenburg pressed the trigger of his Schmeisser. The 9mm slugs ripped his chest open. He sprawled forward, his helmet tumbling over his face, the grenade rolling away harmlessly. Another enemy soldier popped up from a trench which had been dug behind the cover of the manure heap. He had a big pistol in his hand. Schulze kicked him in the face. He screamed and went reeling back, his face a bloody mess.

They rushed on. A smoking halftrack barred the way, dead SS men scattered on the ground all around it in the abandoned postures of the violently-done-to-death. Von Dodenburg sprang over the body of a soldier, whose legs had been ripped off by a burst of heavy machine gun fire at pointblank range.

Two enemy soldiers were trying to mount an ancient Hotchkiss machine gun behind the cover of the smoking halftrack. Their sweat-lathered faces were bent over the gun. Suddenly they saw the advancing SS men. For what seemed an age, their frightened eyes mirrored their indecision. 'Fight or flight' was the question they posed.

Suddenly the bigger of the two dropped the Hotchkiss barrel and began to run. Too late! An SS trooper let him have a burst in the back. He threw up his hands, as if pleading with heaven to spare him, then dropped to the ground on his face without a sound.

The other raised his hands in surrender. But the SS men could not stop themselves now. The bow-legged Bavarian, who had filled his pants during the tank training exercise, fired and the soldier dropped slowly, a look of utter disbelief in his eyes.

Then they were in the burning village. On both sides of the cobbled street, the shattered windows were filled with shouting, firing men. They clattered up the narrow pavements, hugging the protection of the walls, firing upwards. Men dived heavily from the windows and lay sprawled out like broken dolls in the middle of the street.

As they ran on, a big brown Flemish plough horse broke out of a stable, foam bubbling along the line of its slack lips, as it squealed in terror at the flames. A great red ox lumbered after it, thrusting aside a heavy plough, as if it were made of wood.

'The animals, sir!' Schulze yelled above

the noise, his hands cupped around his mouth. He had lost his machine pistol. All he had was a stick grenade thrust into his belt, *'Follow the animals, sir!'*

Von Dodenburg caught on at once. He ran after them as they blundered down the street, sending the defenders scattering to get out of their way. Before they could recover the SS were among them, spraying the streets with lead. The surprised enemy fell back. Men dropped groaning everywhere. Suddenly they broke altogether.

Throwing away their weapons, they scrambled for safety. A wild lust overcame the SS men. They poured burst after burst into the retreating enemy. A group of them jammed a doorway in their frantic attempt to escape. Without mercy the troopers mowed them down. And for good measure, Schulze lobbed a potato masher grenade through the shattered window. It exploded with a muffled crump. From within came pitiful cries of agony, then silence. Slowly a head, with the helmet still attached, came rolling through the door, picking its way through the dead and dying, as if of its own volition. Finally it came to rest at Schulze's feet. He gulped and looked away hurriedly. The crazy moment of murder and mayhem was over.

Slowly the crackle of small arms fire died away, and stopped altogether. Exhausted and drained of all energy they collapsed against the bullet-pocked walls, gasping for breath, as if they had run a great race, their eyes shining wildly, unable to control their shaking limbs. Automatically Kuno von Dodenburg changed the magazine on his Schmeisser and found he had to bite his lips hard and concentrate all his will-power to stop his hands shaking. It was the typical after-action reaction, he knew. Soon, some of the men would begin to cry, for no apparent reason, while others would shake all over, as if affected by a violent fever. Only Geier, appearing suddenly from nowhere, prodding a fat and very frightened Dutch customs sergeant in front of him with his cane, was as calm as ever.

'I found this prime specimen hiding in a barn,' he explained, 'with his fat Dutch arse sticking up from the hay so you could see it a kilometre away.'

The Dutchman was a huge man with a fat pink, well-fed face and a stiff waxed blond moustache of the type favoured by NCOs in the First World War. But that was the only thing martial in his appearance; the tell-tale stain in his grey-green trousers revealed just how much of a coward he was.

'He's pissed himself!' Schulze said contemptuously. 'Just another hero in uniform.'

'Shut up!' the Vulture snarled. 'Our friend here has got some useful information for us.

Haven't you, *Mijnheer?*' He dug the fat official in the small of the back to emphasise his words.

'*Ja, ja, mijnheer,*' he gasped rapidly. 'The tower – the church tower,' he added in guttural German. 'You'll see.'

'Come on, von Dodenburg – and you too, Schwarz,' the Vulture turned to the dark young lieutenant who had just come up, his face black with dirt and powder burns, a rip in his left trouser leg. Rapidly they strode towards the church, with Geier prodding the fat Dutchman in front of him, as if he were herding a pig. Everywhere the young men of the Assault Battalion were beginning to recover from their first taste of action and were rounding up the survivors and a handful of frightened civilians.

Sergeant-Major Metzger appeared, his uniform immaculate; the only sign that he had taken part in the action was the machine pistol clasped in his big fist. He clicked his heels together and reported, as if he were back in the Adolf Hitler Barracks, 'Twenty casualties, sir. Eight dead and twelve wounded, seven seriously, *sir!*'

Geier waved for him to lower his voice. 'See what you can do to patch up the wounded. We'll need every man for the river crossing.'

'Yes, sir,' the Butcher doubled away, his shoulders squared, his weapon carried at exactly a right angle to his big body, just like the soldiers did in the training films.

Geier shook his head. 'No wonder the shitty civilians talk about wooden-headed soldiers.' He prodded the fat Dutchman. 'Come on, we've no time to waste. Every minute counts.'

Schwarz kicked open the door of the church. Cold air greeted them, heavy with the smell of stale incense and unwashed farmers' bodies. A dead soldier lay sprawled across the floor, a rifle still clutched in his hands, his wide-open eyes staring vacantly into nothing. The Dutchman stepped over him carefully. Schwarz, however, gave him a vicious kick in the ribs. 'That bastard got one of my men,' he snarled, 'before we fetched him down from the steeple.'

'Save your energy, my dear Schwarz,' Geier said with a trace of his old cynicism. 'For the living. It is wasted on the dead, believe you me!' He turned to the horrified Dutchman again, who was staring down at the dead soldier. 'Well, *Mijnheer*, where is the best vantage point?'

The Dutchman poked a fat forefinger upwards. 'The tower, sir,' he quavered, 'from there you can see best.'

Von Dodenburg took a step forward, but the Vulture stuck his cane in front of the young officer's chest quickly. 'No, my dear von Dodenburg, you are too good an officer to lose – just yet. In case there are any of our friends still up there, let them have the Mijnheer as their principal target. He's got enough blubber on him to cover the lot of us.' But the platform on top of the tower was empty, save for a handful of white pigeons which flew away as they opened the trap and clambered through.

Cautiously, they crept through one by one, after the Vulture had heaved the fat Dutchman onto the platform with surprising strength for such a small man. The CO glanced around the skyline. The early morning sun was still behind them. He could use his binoculars without their reflection giving away their position. With Schwarz and von Dodenburg flanking him, he crawled to the edge of the platform and peered out. Some five hundred metres away lay a silver snake of silent water stretched out against the background of the deep green fields. Geier looked at them triumphantly. 'Gentlemen, the River Meuse, we have reached objective number one.'

While the Dutchman cowered in the corner, they focused their binoculars carefully and surveyed the river line.

It was Schwarz who spotted the little group of ferry boats tied up to the near bank of the river, downstream of the village. 'Look, sir,' he said, 'boats – six of them. Enough to get half the company across in one go.'

But before Geier had time to express his

approval, von Dodenburg cut in. 'Yes, and the position is covered by enemy infantry. Can you see, sir? At ten o'clock – two groups of them, among those bushes. Looks as if they've got a machine gun too. It's obvious that it's a well-known crossing point and they're prepared for anyone who might make the attempt.'

From below came the sound of Sergeant-Major Metzger's voice, as he lined up the villagers and the captured troops, giving them orders in pigeon German, which he presumably thought they would understand as long as it was shouted loud enough and supported by a few well-directed blows.

'Idiot!' the Vulture grunted. 'Why doesn't he shut his stupid face? I can't think with that row going on.'

Schwarz leaned over the parapet, as if he were about to transmit the CO's complaint to the Sergeant-Major but he stopped and turned back to them.

'I have an idea, sir. Those men dug in over there are Belgians, but they have a common language with the villagers. They might even have girl friends over here. You know what soldiers are – and the border is only a stretch of water.'

'What are you getting at?'

'Well, sir, would they fire on the villagers, that's the point?' Swiftly he explained his plan.

122

'Capital,' Geier exclaimed, 'a capital idea, Schwarz!' He slapped him on the back enthusiastically. 'Of course, it'll work!'

'But sir,' von Dodenburg protested, 'they're civilians. You couldn't...' he broke off, at a loss to find the right words to express his outrage.

The Vulture looked at him coldly. 'My dear von Dodenburg, what terrible scruples you have for an SS officer! Don't you realise that a whole army is lining up behind us and behind that a whole nation of eighty million souls? In the face of that, what is important or even significant about the lives of a few obscure civilians?'

He did not allow time for any further protest. 'Come on,' he snapped, 'let's go. Time is running out!' He rose to his feet and clattered over the platform to the stone steps. Behind them the sun was high on the horizon now, blood-red and ominous, a portent of the blood-letting to come.

CHAPTER TWO

An ominous silence lay over the broad expanse of the river. Grimly they herded the terrified group of Dutch civilians towards the boats. At first the fat Sergeant helped them.

123

He had confided to them that 'as a member of the Dutch Fascist Movement' he 'sympathised with the German cause'. But now that he realised he was to go with the rest, he fell on his knees in the mud of the river bank, and hands held up in supplication, tears pouring down his fat face, he pleaded with them to let him go. A tall skinny boy, who did not look a day over sixteen, spat scornfully and said in fair German, 'What a good friend you have found to help you!'

Schwarz hit the boy hard across the face. 'Shut your dirty mouth,' he cried.

The terrified civilians were soon pushed into the boats and made to pick up the oars. A couple of SS men got in behind them, where they knew they would be safe. Geier, who had posted half the company along the bank around the crossing point, looked at von Dodenburg. 'All right?' he asked.

'Yes sir,' von Dodenburg snapped. A little voice deep down within his brain was crying out in protest, but he did not listen to it and when, in years to come, he began to pay attention to it, it was too late.

'Good. Let's get on with it then.'

Von Dodenburg barked out an order.

The first boat pushed off. Immediately, half a dozen SS men, their boots tied around their necks, their weapons held high in their right hands, slipped into the water after it and grasped its sides.

One by one the other boats followed until half the company was in the water, with von Dodenburg commanding the right wing and Schwarz, the originator of the plan, the left. There was no sound, save the rusty squeak of the oars wielded by the civilians and, in the distance, the low rumble of artillery, the ever-present background music of war.

Von Dodenburg, swimming easily, kept his eyes firmly fixed on the opposite bank. Nothing stirred. Perhaps Schwarz's plan might work without bloodshed after all. They were halfway across now and he could see every detail of the far bank quite clearly – the wet line of the mud, the rusty strands of barbed wire and the tense faces of the soldiers who had crawled close to the bank to meet this strange invasion.

Suddenly a red flare soared into the sky and hung momentarily over the river. As it hissed into the water, a Belgian officer in gleaming riding boots rose from the grass and cupping his hands to his mouth, yelled, *'Terug!'* The civilians stopped rowing immediately. 'Major,' the fat sergeant quavered, 'they'll shoot. Turn back, please!'

'Carry on!' von Dodenburg bellowed. 'See they keep moving, men!'

The men in the boats needed no urging. Every yard gained, they knew, was one further towards dry land and safety. They jabbed their weapons into the backs of the terrified men and women. The boats moved forward again.

Von Dodenburg could see the awful indecision mirrored in the Belgian officer's face. Should he order his men to fire and prevent the Germans crossing the vital waterway? Or should he attempt to save the civilians and sacrifice his position.

Desperately he cried: *'Terug, als'tu blieft!'*

'Keep 'em going,' von Dodenburg warned, knowing that he was signing the civilians' death warrant.

In the leading boat, the two SS men tensed for the landing. Von Dodenburg could see the bow-legged Bavarian who had slaughtered the surrendering Dutch soldier raise his machine pistol ready for action. They were only a matter of ten years from the Belgian officer now. They had almost done it.

Suddenly the blond boy, whom Schwarz had struck, sprang to his feet. The boat shook dangerously with the violence of his movement. *'Shoot!'* he yelled in Dutch, *'Shoot the bastards!'*

His cry seemed to break the spell. The Belgian officer ducked as a machine gun began to chatter. The first burst caught the boy in the chest and he fell to the bottom of the boat. Behind him the Bavarian raised his machine pistol. A burst struck him in the face. Screaming with pain, he fell over the side.

'*Attack!*' von Dodenburg yelled. '*Attack!*'
Grabbing Schulze, he pulled him away
from the boat and struck out for the bank.
Lead hissed over the water, but by now the
SS men were already scrambling up the
bank in safety, while the machine gun
turned the boats into a bloody mess of dead
and dying civilians.

Schulze ran forward towards the Belgian
positions, his entrenching tool his only
weapon. His mouth wide open, screaming
terrible obscenities, he flung himself on the
Belgians. A big soldier who had the red,
weathered face of a farmer tackled him. With
all his strength Schulze brought his shovel
down. Its sharp blade cleaved into the Belgian's face. He screamed like a stuck pig. A
great slice of his face came away with the
shovel. He dropped, drowning in his own
blood.

The officer crashed into von Dodenburg.
They grappled with each other. Then von
Dodenburg jerked his knee into the man's
groin and he screamed and staggered back,
clasping his stomach. Von Dodenburg fired
a full burst into him, the slugs at such short
range throwing him off his feet and carrying
him a good two yards.

A helmetless Belgian sprang on to Kuno's
back. The bayonet which he held like a knife
glanced off the leather strap over von
Dodenburg's shoulder. He rolled over,

127

dragging the man with him. In grim silence, they struggled together on the grass. With all his strength the Belgian stabbed downwards. Von Dodenburg swung his head to one side at the very last moment. The Belgian cursed hotly in Flemish and tried to draw out his bayonet. Schulze towered over him, his entrenching tool raised high above his head, its blade gleaming with blood. The next instant it bit deep into the back of the Fleming's skull which split in two. The Belgian rolled on his back dead.

Then, as suddenly as it had started, the hand-to-hand struggle was over, the Belgian survivors running wildly into the fields beyond, flinging their weapons away in their haste to escape, while a couple of SS troopers fired wild bursts after them.

The 2nd Company, SS Assault Battalion Wotan had crossed the River Meuse, the first of the great obstacles in their way, at the cost of exactly two dead and four slightly wounded. But behind them the water was heavy with the bodies of dead civilians.

'Excellent, excellent,' Geier chortled, as he stepped out of the boat. 'A tremendous achievement. There'd be a piece of tin in this for you, von Dodenburg and you, too, Schwarz, but for that unfortunate business back there.' He indicated the bodies in the water behind him. 'I'm afraid that wouldn't look too pretty in the recommendation.' He cast a quick look at the slaughtered soldiers, sprawled everywhere in the gory shambles of the trenches. 'Poor equipment,' he commented. 'Look, they've still got the old 1916 model water-cooled Vickers! I thought that type was ripe for the museum.' He stepped over the body of the dead officer, whose pockets stuck up stiffly, where someone had looted their contents. 'They could have done a better job with their emplacement too, don't you think?'

Only Schwarz had the energy to reply. 'Inferior types, sir,' he breathed, as if he were still having trouble in obtaining enough air. 'Racially, that is.'

'Just so,' the Vulture assented, and dismissed the dead and Schwarz's genetic theories. Glancing at his watch, he announced. 'We have got exactly twenty-five hours left, gentlemen. So far we have done exceedingly well. I congratulate you all. But that is now history. Beyond that next rise you can see up there is the village of Canne. Possibly their paratroopers have made a crossing of the Albert Canal. My guess is that they will have failed to do so. I think you all know my opinion of the Luftwaffe.'

'You mean we will have to cross the Canal by force, sir?' Fick asked. Blood was still seeping through the thick field dressing bound round his wounded arm.

'Yes, I'm afraid that King Leopold won't send his royal yacht to ferry us across,' the Vulture said cynically.

'But we shall worry about that in due course. Our first problem is to get into Canne. Fick, you'll stay at the river and guard the crossing with Kaufmann.' The latter was still on the far bank trying to raise Battalion on the radio to inform Major Hartmann of their tremendous coup.

Fick pulled a face, but his arm was hurting like hell and he did not protest.

'You, Schwarz,' the Vulture continued, 'will approach the village from the south. And you,' he turned to von Dodenburg, 'from the north. I'll follow up with half a platoon in reserve. Whoever makes the breakthrough sends a runner back to inform me at once. We'll throw in the bulk of the company then. After all, remember the old Prussian motto – *Klotzen nicht klecksen?*' He caught the look on Schwarz's face, one of sudden dramatic animation. 'And my dear Schwarz, let us have no theatre! Your throat-ache will be cured in due course. You've already earned the Iron Cross – first class. Be content and save your men. We need every one of them.'

Schwarz's eyes lit up at the mention of the coveted award. 'You mean that, sir?'

'Naturally, I always say what I mean. You shall have your piece of tin in due course; *if*

130

you survive,' the Vulture added *sotto voice.*

If the Lieutenant heard, his face did not show it. All it betrayed was a fierce determination to carry out the Vulture's orders, spurred on by the promise of the decoration.

'Stupid fool,' the Vulture thought to himself. 'For a piece of tin, he'd march to the moon and back!'

But he didn't express his thoughts aloud. He contented himself with a brisk military, 'Well, gentlemen, get to it and happy landings!'

'Is there anything you can do for him?' von Dodenburg asked, as Schulze bent over the Dutch boy, whom he had fished out of the water.

Schulze did not answer at once. He was busy taking off the boy's blood-soaked shirt, without causing more pain than he had to. For such a big man, he had surprisingly gentle hands. All the same the boy groaned. His breath was coming in short, shallow gasps, his eyes flickered open, wet with pain. His chest, now free, was a gory mess. Through the holes made by the first burst of machine gun bullets, they could see something white against the gleaming red, which jerked back and forth tremulously.

'His lungs,' Schulze said in a whisper.

The boy heard the word and understood. 'The lungs,' he said weakly. 'So. The Belgians can shoot better than you German bastards at least.' His head fell back, as if he accepted his fate, knowing that there was nothing more to be said or done.

Slowly Schulze got to his feet. He wiped his hands on the sides of his trousers. 'He's a brave little bastard,' he said, almost as if he were speaking to himself. Then his voice rose and he looked at von Dodenburg. 'What are we going to do with him, Lieutenant?'

Von Dodenburg looked down at the dying boy. 'Get yourself a weapon and join the rest.' He indicted the waiting SS men, not taking his eyes off the Dutch boy.

Reluctantly Schulze did as he was told, casting a curious look over his shoulder a couple of times. The Butcher snapped an order and they began to trudge up the slope in the direction of the village. Schulze breasted the height. Stretched in front of them were the gleaming green fields, shimmering now as the sun burnt away the dew. Beyond they could make out the flat dumpy outline of the village of Canne.

A lone pistol shot rang out behind the column. He turned and saw von Dodenburg running to catch up with them, the flap of his holster springing up and down as he ran. He didn't look at Schulze as he joined the column. They plodded on.

132

CHAPTER THREE

The village of Canne was fleeing.

Like their fathers, twenty-six years before, the men of Canne and their families were running west. The Prussians were coming yet once again!

To the SS men crouched in the drainage ditch surveying the western exit to the little village, it seemed as if all the stables and barns in the place had opened their doors to spew forth their contents on to the road. Great, open-sided farm carts, drawn by huge red oxen or ancient nags; dog carts, made of wicker-work, with Alsatian dogs padding beneath them; bicycles; wheel-barrows; even an invalid chair, powered by a blue-smoking, two-stroke motor. Everything and anything which could move, all packed high with the villagers' pathetic bits and pieces, mixed with their animals. There was even a barefoot boy, his shoes tied round his neck to save the precious shoe leather, beating forward a flock of protesting geese.

'Christ on the cross!' Schulze breathed softly, 'I bet they've got the kitchen sink with them too!'

'You could be...'

Von Dodenburg broke off suddenly. A double file of cyclists were forcing its way through the panic-stricken refugees, trying desperately to keep up some kind of military formation.

'The Frontier Cyclists!' he exclaimed in amazement.

'Oh, my aching arse!' Schulze said. 'Would you believe it! Don't the poor arseholes know there's a war on?'

Apparently they didn't.

Stolidly, the brown-clad cyclists, their rifles slung over their backs, rode up the centre of the road, scattering the civilians, as if they were on a routine patrol. One of them waved to a pretty girl herding a couple of goats.

Von Dodenburg tapped the butt of his magazine to check if it were correctly fitted and the Butcher, who was crouched at his right, looked at him nervously. 'Are you going to attack them, sir?' he asked, his voice strangely distorted.

Von Dodenburg stared at him curiously. 'Of course, Sergeant-Major, they're a sitting target.'

'But what if they're a come-on, sir?' the Butcher protested. 'It's too easy. I think we should let them go by and then move in on the village.'

Von Dodenburg realised then just how much of a coward Sergeant-Major Metzger was and made a mental note to talk to

Captain Geier about it as soon as the action was over. 'You might,' he said icily, 'but I don't.'

'Of course, of course, sir,' the Butcher agreed hastily. 'It was just a suggestion.'

Von Dodenburg ignored him. 'Schulze, pass the word on. As soon as I fire, everyone is to join in. Not one of them is to escape.'

'And the civvies?' Schulze asked softly.

Von Dodenburg did not answer.

The cyclists came closer. Von Dodenburg counted them. Nearly a hundred. They outnumbered his men by two to one. But that didn't matter; they had surprise on their side.

A farm dog began to bark at the legs of the leading soldier. Without changing his erect posture or taking his eyes off the road, he launched a kick at it. The dog ran off howling. They were only fifty yards away now.

Von Dodenburg raised his machine pistol and focused on the man who had kicked the dog. He had a pompous pale face; he looked more like some jumped-up clerk than a soldier. The pale face began to fill the centre of his foresight. He fired and a row of red holes appeared along the man's breast. For one moment he continued to pedal on. Then he flung up his arms.

The next instant the others joined in. At once all was panic-stricken confusion. Animals broke away and burst the fences on both sides of the road. Refugees screamed and fled after them. In vain the cyclists tried to unsling their weapons, but the concealed SS men gave them no chance. Mercilessly they mowed them down.

Von Dodenburg rose to his feet, shouting 'Follow me!' Sergeant-Major Metzger was first to spring up after him. Together they ran forward, firing from the hip as they ran. The rest followed, pouring a hail of bullets into the confused, chaotic press of soldiers and civilians fighting to get away from the site of the massacre.

In a matter of seconds it was over. Dead and wounded lay everywhere. Ahead, from the village, came the sound of firing, the unmistakeable high-pitched burr of a German spandau. It was obvious that Lieutenant Schwarz and his men had run into trouble.

Schwarz, his head bleeding and a biting pain in his side, sat crouched in the evil-smelling farm privy and cursed. It had all been too easy. He had doubled his men forward into the village. Nothing had stirred. Confidently, his mind full of Captain Geier's 'piece of tin', he had ordered them to advance without any preliminary reconnaissance. One of his NCOs, 'old hole-in-the-arse', as the men called him, had protested. But he had overridden his protests. 'You can see they're running away, Sergeant,' he had shouted triumphantly, pointing at the refugees streaming out of the village. 'Those Belgies have creamed their pants for sure!' He had waved to the troopers crouching on both sides of the road, and like some hero in a UFA film, had shouted 'Advance!'

A moment later the slow Belgian machine gun had opened up from the first of the abandoned cottages. 'Hole-in-the-arse' had gone down. This time the holes had been final. Schwarz watched horrified as half his force melted away under the withering enemy fire.

Now he was trapped in the privy, to which he had crawled while the survivors of his group had fled down the road, abandoning their dying comrades, concerned only in escaping from that terrible wall of lead. Every time he raised his head, a bullet whacked into the stones above.

Schwarz wiped away the blood which was dripping from his wounded forehead and took stock of his situation as rationally as he could. It seemed as if he were alone in the village, though somewhere in the distance he could make out the high-pitched burr of German automatic weapons. But that was far away and he could hear nothing from the direction of his original position. His men had either fled or were sprawled out dead along the road.

Desperately he racked his brains for some way out of the mess he had got himself into. He knew that the Vulture would never forgive him for losing so many men when their objective was still not taken. The Vulture's bourgeois mentality would ensure that he was posted to some rear echelon outfit, where he would remain a 'base stallion' for the rest of war, while others won the decorations. In a year's time when the war was over, there would be 20-year-old captains, even majors, flashing around their knight's crosses, and he would still be a lieutenant, long overdue for promotion, his only decoration the War Service Cross, the medal they gave to fat-arsed civilian war workers.

Schwarz squirmed round on his back and fumbled in his breast pocket for his metal shaving mirror, which he had put there to protect his heart. Taking care not to let it reflect the sun's rays, he raised it slowly above his head. Half a dozen bodies in German uniform came into view, sprawled out on the *pavé* like broken dolls. They were his own men. He bit his lip and levered the mirror up a little more.

From the broken window of the first little cottage opposite his hiding place, the barrel of a Belgian machine gun poked threateningly. He swung the mirror to the right and caught a glimpse of another gun muzzle and a white face behind it. And another. The

Belgian bastards certainly had him by the short and curlies.

Suddenly in the sky away to the east he saw a black gull-like shape. It was a long way away, but Schwarz recognised it immediately. 'A Junkers 87,' he cried aloud. 'And another!' There was no mistaking their strange angular shapes, as the Luftwaffe's most deadly weapon droned closer and closer to the village.

As the noise of the engines grew louder by the second, Schwarz fumbled feverishly for his signal pistol. Hastily he fitted the first cartridge into the pistol, hoping he could remember the right order of colours to summon the aircraft.

He took another hurried glance at them through the mirror. Now they were flying low, perhaps two hundred metres at the most, keeping perfect formation, completely ignoring the tracer zipping in their direction.

Schwarz raised his pistol and, without exposing his body, fired in the direction of the Belgians. A red flare hissed into the sky. From across the road there came angry shouts. Bullets whined through the air. Above his head the door splintered and showered him with chips of wood. He fired again. A white flare sailed out in a great curve and hung over the Belgian positions. Then it slowly began to fall.

Schwarz waited. Had they seen his signal?

And if so, had they understood it? He felt the sweat trickle down the small of his back, and he realised that he might have signed his own death warrant.

Then it started. The leading plane, completely black save for its yellow spinner, seemed to stop in mid-air. Its pilot tilted it sharply to port. Schwarz caught a glimpse of the black-and-white cross on its port wing. Suddenly, without any warning whatsoever, it appeared to fall out of the sky – a black stone plummeting down against the blue background.

The pilot turned on his sirens, which Schwarz remembered so well from the newsreels of the Polish fighting. Their bloodcurdling scream filled the air. He clapped his hands to his ears to cut out the tremendous noise.

One hundred and fifty, one hundred, seventy metres, then the pilot levelled out. Dozens of bombs shining in the sunlight, came falling from its belly, jostling each other as they wobbled down towards the Belgian positions.

The incendiaries ignited, throwing out tiny pellets of magnesium everywhere. Within a matter of seconds thick, stinking clouds of white smoke had enveloped the houses. Someone screamed and a Belgian soldier burst through the smoke, his uniform already alight. He zig-zagged up the littered street, the flames licking higher and higher up his body. Schwarz waited no longer. Tossing aside the flare pistol, he flung open the door of the privy. A bullet smacked into the wall a yard away. Brick splinters splattered his face. Already the first of the houses opposite was beginning to burn fiercely. The Belgies would have no time for him now. The super-heated air seared at his lungs. Frantically he glanced up and down the street, looking for a way out.

Above him, beyond the thick pall of white smoke, a second Stuka was beginning its dive, its sirens going full out. He spotted the church. He knew that the *Luftwaffe,* like the artillery, had orders to avoid damaging enemy churches – 'cultural wealth' – as they were called in standing orders.

Gasping for air, he started to run for it. The screaming roar of the Stuka grew louder and louder. Suddenly the roar stopped and was replaced by a sinister, high-pitched whistle. *High explosive!*

Desperately Schwarz flung himself at the great wooden door of the church, clutching for the iron handle. As the first bomb exploded the door sagged open and he fell inside to confront a little man who crouched there in the incense-heavy darkness.

The helmetless SS man came running down the grassy slope, arms flailing, eyes wild with fear, meaningless sounds coming from his mouth. An NCO struck at him with his fist. He side-stepped and kept on running. The Butcher cursed angrily and as the panic-stricken soldier came level with him, he jammed the butt of his machine-pistol into his face. The SS man dropped to the ground, shivering like a young puppy.

He was the first of a dozen or so survivors of Lieutenant Schwarz's group whom the Butcher lined up in front of von Dodenburg with the aid of his levelled machine pistol. With a nod of his head, von Dodenburg indicated that he should lower the weapon. For a moment he said nothing; just looked at their white faces, their eyes staring and blank.

'What happened?' he asked the first man.

The soldier opened his mouth, but no sound came.

He asked the next man who began to babble a confused explanation. He slapped him hard across the face. The man staggered back, then shook his head a couple of times like someone waking up from a deep sleep. Von Dodenburg lowered his hand to his pistol. 'I'll give you three,' he said, 'and if you haven't started giving me a rational answer by then, I'll kill you.'

Von Dodenburg's men gasped with shock. Of all the officers in Battalion, he was the only one who never used his hands on the enlisted men. This sudden display of brutality was completely unexpected. But, as von Dodenburg had expected, the soldier began to talk, his description of what had happened in Canne coming in short hurried gasps. As he listened, the young officer felt his anger at Schwarz's foolishness begin to burn within him. It was typical of the spirit that the Vulture had engendered within the 2nd Company. 'Forward over the bodies' was his motto – one that had been swallowed hook, line and sinker by ambitious young fools like Schwarz. And what a mess he had landed himself in with it!

But there was no time now to dwell on Geier's theories. He would have to try to take the village without Schwarz's aid. Just as the Stukas came howling in over the little cluster of houses around the church, he began to give his orders.

'My name is Weissfisch,' the little man said with surprising formality, as the Stukas flew away, 'Moishe Weissfisch.'

Schwarz, his left hand clutching his right arm in an attempt to stem the flow of blood from his wound, stared at the civilian in horror. With a name like that, he had to be a Jew. He was alone in a dark little Belgian church with a Yid!

The man seemed to read his thoughts. 'Yes, Lieutenant,' he said in excellent German, 'I am a Jew.'

'But you speak German – and how did you know I am a lieutenant?'

The civilian smiled sadly. 'Because I am as much a German as you,' he answered.

'You're not a German!' he cried. 'You are a Jew!'

Weissfisch nodded. 'Of course, but for fifty odd years of my life I paid my taxes, did my job, honoured my nation in the belief that I was part of it.' He held up his right hand. It was encased in a dark-brown leather glove. 'Verdun 1916,' he said in explanation.

'And what are you doing now here, Jew?' Schwarz snapped.

Weissfisch shrugged. 'Like the fool I've been all my life, Lieutenant, I stayed on. I believed that things might change, that all the hate against the Jews would cease when Germany had regained what she lost at Versailles. A week ago after they came to take away my wife – according to your strange classification of humanity, she was something called "full-Jew" – I decided to cross the Belgian border.' He smiled, the look on his face a mixture of sadness and self-contempt. 'As you can see, it seems I am too late.' He broke off suddenly and looked at Schwarz curiously. 'But haven't I seen you somewhere before?' he asked.

'Me? How the hell would a Jew like you know me?' Schwarz cried. 'You must be crazy!' A horrible realisation started to grow within him, as the little Jew stared at him with no apparent fear. 'Can't you see the runes on my collar? What would I be doing with racial dirt like you?'

'Forgive me, Lieutenant,' the Jew persisted. 'But your face. Those eyes...'

'Shut up!' Schwarz shouted at him.

But the little Jew wouldn't stop talking. With almost masochistic relish, he warmed to his subject. 'In these last seven years, Lieutenant, I've had ample opportunity to study your National Socialist racial theories, and you know, I think there is something in them. In the Great War we always used to laugh at the "Polack noses" of the recruits from West Prussia, and in the Rhineland you can always tell a "Frankish face". A fat pudding with a carrot of a nose stuck in the middle of it. Now your face, Lieutenant, exhibits the typical characteristics of the Central European Jew...' The little man's words stopped suddenly, as Schwarz grabbed him by the throat, his face masked in hate, his lips drawn back in an inhuman snarl like a trapped animal. 'How dare you, a Jew, a Jew,' he breathed hoarsely, too shocked to be able to formulate the sentence necessary to ward off the monstrous accusation. Instead he pushed him hard against the bare white-washed wall.

The little man stared up at him. There was

145

no fear in his eyes only sadness and compassion, as he prepared to meet the inevitable.

Schwarz's rage at the trick fate had played on him exploded within him. With all his strength he squeezed the Jew's skinny neck. Weissfisch's eyes bulged and his tongue shot out of his mouth. But he made no attempt to protect himself.

Deaf to the renewed rattle of gunfire, blind to everything but the Jew's face, he crushed the life out of his body until it gave one final violent contortion and was still for good.

Together they fell to the floor of the church, Schwarz's shoulders heaving as if he were sobbing, his head bent on the dead Jew's breast like a son asking his father's forgiveness for some unforgivable crime.

The men of von Dodenburg's group found him barricaded in the door of the church, a couple of ancient Lebel rifles on the pews he had used as cover, his machine pistol clasped in his hands, peering at the Belgians he had shot, sprawled out dead in the churchyard.

'Good for you, sir!' they cried enthusiastically, raising their helmets and wiping the sweat from their brows. 'You really showed the bastards!'

One of them who had run away came over and apologised to him. 'Sorry, sir. But it was the first time in action and...'

Schwarz waved aside his protestations.

'It's all right, man.'

Kuno von Dodenburg pushed the man aside and leaned warily at the door, breathed out hard and said: 'What happened to him?' He indicated the little civilian slumped in the corner, his head bent at an impossible angle, bloody scratches down both sides of his sallow face, as if a wild animal had worked on him.

Schwarz did not even bother to look at the dead Jew. 'Don't know,' he said tonelessly. 'Some civvie, I suppose.' He shrugged carelessly. 'Killed in the initial assault. Who knows?'

Von Dodenburg looked at Schwarz curiously. There was something strange about him. He had lost half his force, had been cut off for over two hours and had fought off the best part of a Belgian platoon single-handed. Yet he was utterly calm. And there was something far-away, vague, almost crazy about his eyes. There was not even the suspicion of a tremor in the hand that lit the cigarette which Sergeant-Major Metzger offered him so respectfully. He looked from Schwarz back to the little civilian slumped in the corner. No sign of a bullet wound. And where had those strange scratches come from?

But von Dodenburg had no time to investigate the matter further. From outside came the chug-chug of an ancient engine, followed by the hoarse cheers of the tired young men lolling around in the square outside. He swung round and, followed by the officious Butcher, went hurriedly outside.

It was Geier and his reserve, crowded into an old Ford truck, piled high with equipment. Even before it stopped, Geier sprang out of the cab and came hurrying over them, his face beaming. 'Gentlemen, Major Hartmann has been seriously wounded and the rest of the Battalion has suffered serious losses on the Meuse. I am to take over the Battalion for the time being.' He slapped his cane against the side of his boot. Von Dodenburg looked at Schwarz. But the latter's face was still numb and expressionless.

'I see, sir,' was all that von Dodenburg could say, in the face of such naked pleasure at the realization of his ambition.

'Break out the cognac and cigars,' he shouted at the men on the truck. 'For everybody!'

There was a whoop of joy from Von Dodenburg's weary men. They hurried forward, while the soldiers on the truck handed down their equipment, followed by boxes of looted Dutch cigars.

'Kaufmann found them,' the Vulture said, beaming. 'He ferried them across with the equipment. They came at a very opportune time to celebrate my promotion, eh?' He looked at von Dodenburg, as if it were only natural that he should share his joy, although it had been gained at the cost of so much human suffering. 'Of course it's only temporary, but who knows what the next few hours may bring, eh?' Then his face was serious again. 'All right, you and you Schwarz, let's get up to the water and have a look at Fort Eben-Emael.'

While the men of SS Assault Battalion Wotan celebrated with the looted cognac, the three officers set off across the fields towards the last barrier between them and Europe's greatest fortress.

CHAPTER FOUR

A paratroop helmet with a jagged hole in it lay in the grass just in front of von Dodenburg's nose. Inside the sweat band he could make out its owner's name quite clearly. 'Para-Corporal Horst Küfer'. Soon, he thought, a telegram would be hurrying to his next-of-kin to inform them that he had 'died for Folk and Führer'. Behind them, as they lay surveying the canal, one of the great DFS gliders which had brought the paras was sprawled out in a copse of snapped-off firs like a broken butterfly; there was no sign of its occupants, only the sound of German automatic weapons coming from some-where in the cloud of smoke which enveloped Fort Eben-Emael.

'They're still up there somewhere,' Geier said, staring at the stretch of the Albert Canal, with the almost sheer concrete wall rising beyond. 'That's something.' His initial elation at his temporary promotion had vanished as soon as he had seen the Canal and the wall beyond and had realized the magnitude of the task facing them.

Von Dodenburg focused his binoculars on the smashed bridge downstream. The shattered girders which hung drunkenly into the water were littered with the grey-smocked bodies of the paras who had failed to capture it before the Belgians had blown it up. 'They've got two m.g. positions covering it, as far as I can make out, sir. And there's a twin Oerlikon in that little copse beyond it at two o'clock.'

The Vulture nodded his understanding. 'Yes, I can see it. At least this spot appears not to be...'

One of the hidden fort's great cannon spoke. The fog of war was parted by a stab of red flame. A moment later it was followed by a sound like canvas being torn apart. A monstrous shell, so big that at first they could actually see it, hurtled through the air, bound for the German troops massed far to the rear.

'Thank God for that,' Geier continued. 'The paras haven't succeeded in knocking out the gun emplacements yet. I was worried that they might have been able to do so with their damned hollow charges.'

Von Dodenburg looked at him, open-mouthed. The Vulture had made the statement as if it were the most obvious thing in the world. He shook his head in amazement and then dismissed his CO's overweening ambition; there was nothing he could do about it. 'What are your orders, sir?' he asked dutifully.

The Vulture put down his glasses and looked at his wristwatch. 'God in heaven!' he cursed. 'It's already fifteen hundred hours. We've only got eighteen left for the link-up.'

'The men are beat,' von Dodenburg said. 'They must have a rest.'

'I know, I know,' Geier snapped. 'I know how much the men can stand.'

'Sorry, sir.'

Geier waved his hand hastily, as if the matter were not worth any further discussion. 'This spot is as good as any. We cross as soon as the sun goes down. Seventeen hundred at the latest. Understood?'

'Yes, sir.'

'The men can rest till then. In the meantime I shall go back to Battalion and get it moving again. If you can get across I'll back you up with every man I can find.'

'Sir,' Schwarz broke in hoarsely, speaking for the first time. *'Look!'*

He pointed across the canal, beyond the steep glacis wall to the great grey-black mass of the fort which had suddenly appeared in the midst of the smoke, drifting into view like some huge ship emerging from a fog-bank. It rose like a massive concrete cliff, some two hundred and fifty feet above the water of the canal, its sides covered with ports as in an old man-of-war, but the guns they contained were no puny eight pounders; they were mighty 75mm cannon, mounted in pairs, and covered by supporting machine guns. For one long moment Fort Eben-Emael stood there, sinister and silent; then it slid slowly out of view again, disappearing into the grey fog of war.

While the men slept in the wrecked village, the Butcher prowled, sleepless and miserable, through the deserted streets. Although he was as tired as the rest of the men of the 2nd Company, worry drove him out to wander aimlessly through the wreckage, his mind full of the threat posed by von Dodenburg and the crossing of the Albert Canal, due in a couple of hours.

Idly he kicked a Belgian helmet in front of him in a highly unmilitary manner, taking a sip at his bottle of cognac after every five kicks. He had never imagined that war would be like this, in spite of the fact that he had spent the last ten years of his life preparing for combat. The day did not end at seventeen hundred hours, as in the barracks, and the men were not alert and clean, but dirty, disgruntled and disrespectful. It was the attitude of the officers that displeased him most, especially that of von Dodenburg. Back in the Adolf Hitler Barracks, he had always known that without him nothing functioned; that the officers had relied upon him implicitly to ensure that the men, lazy, dirty bastards that they were, did as they were told – got up on time, washed, entered their names in the bath-book, cleaned their rifles and their foreskins at the prescribed intervals, in short, tried to be soldiers and not dirty-arsed, fornicating civilians. But here at the front everything was different.

Suddenly not only was he superfluous, he was also suspected of being a coward: he, a man, who had been known to 'make a sow' of a whole company in his heyday, who had once spotted that a recruit had not polished his belt buckle at a distance of fifty yards, and who in 1936 had been complimented on his ability to do the parade march by no less a person than Reichsführer Heinrich Himmler himself! Suddenly green-beaks like Mr Senior Lieutenant Shit von Dodenburg could accuse *him* of cowardice!

As if he hadn't enough trouble as it was!

Tears of self-pity sprang to his eyes as he thought of what Lore had said to him, just after he had blacked her eye and knocked out several teeth on the night of his visit to the shitty-arsed rural quack. *He had never been able to satisfy her in all the ten years of their married life!* He took another sip of cognac.

Any woman who thought like that must be a whore of the lowest class. What decent woman concerned herself with such things? Orgasm, she called it, whatever that might be. In his hey-day, before he had married Lore and taken her out of the cafe to bring her up to his own status, he had been keeping four women happy, including one who was 'in hope' and wanted to do it all the time, as well as a doctor's wife – and everybody knows what they are like in bed, thanks to the perverted training they get from their husbands!

Sergeant-Major Metzger kicked the helmet and missed, staggering drunkenly and almost falling over. So now he had a terrible disease and no one cared. How would Mr Senior Lieutenant Shit von Dodenburg like to have his cock wrapped up in a little calico bag and hurting like hell every time he pissed and still be expected to go into action? He wouldn't like it one little bit! Drunkenly the Sergeant-Major grinned at himself in the glass of a shop window and mimed the word 'No'.

Then he frowned at himself, martially. Captain Geier was different. He was not one of these wartime shits. He was an old pre-war soldier, who knew what the old days had been like – hard and unyielding. If you told a recruit to go and shit in his helmet, he would go and shit in it, even if he had to take senna pods to do so. His little red eyes filled with tears again at the memory of the old days.

'Those were good days, believe you me,' he said severely to his image in the window, swaying wildly. 'Soldiers were soldiers then, not shitty green beaks...'

He broke off suddenly. Another figure was standing beside him, staring at the glass, a crazy smile on her broad face. He turned, his hand on the trigger of his pistol. A girl was standing there, her bare legs stuck in huge manure-stained wooden clogs, her body covered in a dirty flowered peasant overall, with her mousy-blonde hair tied up in two absurd plaits that stuck out on both sides of her gaping face like wings. But the Butcher's drunken eyes were focused on her huge breasts which threatened to burst out of the skimpy overall every time she breathed, 'Oh my aching back,' he breathed in respectful awe, 'haven't you got a lot of wood in front of the door!' The idiot girl grinned stupidly, revealing that both her front upper teeth were missing. She opened her thick legs and thrust out her plump stomach in unmistak-

155

able invitation, her mouth open and slack with desire.

The drunken Sergeant-Major felt an immediate stirring of lust at the idiot girl's directness, her blatant wantonness.

The girl recognised the look in his blurred red eyes immediately. *'Ik heet Anna. Ik ben niet getrouwd,'* she said slowly, her lips having difficulty in forming the simple words. The Butcher did not understand a word, but he did understand the unmistakable gesture she made with her thumb and two fingers.

'Where?'

She curled a dirty finger at him. *'Komm.'*

He staggered after her through the rubble. They turned off into a little cobbled lane. She opened the door of a dirty white cottage. It was dark and smelled of animals and sour milk. An ancient sagging brass bed stood in one corner, with a white chamber pot underneath it. It was full. The Butcher looked away hastily.

With a little scream of delight the idiot girl flung herself on the bed. It squeaked in protest. She grinned stupidly and her crazy eyes gleamed with lust. *'Nix vader, nix moeder,'* she said and indicted with a wave of her hand that they had fled with the rest of the village. *'Heel goed!'*

The Butcher waited no longer. With the back of his boot he kicked the door closed.

On the bed, the mad girl opened her legs. He saw she was naked. She threw her legs up in an importuning arch. The Butcher sensed his breath coming in rapid gasps. He hesitated. If he did it, the girl would get the disease. She moaned, put her hand between her legs and moved her powerful thighs in an unmistakable gesture.

The Butcher hesitated no longer. What did it matter with an idiot? Besides the whole world was against him. What did he care? With fumbling fingers, he tore at his flies. On the bed the girl squealed in anticipation. Drunkenly he fell on top of her. Her tongue penetrated his open mouth. For a moment her stale, unwashed smell repelled him. But then she pressed her tongue deep into his mouth and sucked at his saliva greedily, and he soon forgot the war, his problems, everything. Like a blind man, his big hands sought and found her great puddings of breasts.

Solemnly and in utter silence Lieutenant von Dodenburg moved from body to body removing the identity discs and fumbling in pockets for the dead men's few personal possessions: a photograph of a girlfriend or mother; the patiently written letter from a father urging caution and duty; that of a mother full of love and concern; one or two grubby low denomination mark notes. Behind him Schulze wrote down the names on a piece of paper with a stub of pencil, squinting in the rapidly failing light.

Von Dodenburg sighed and straightened up above the dead body of a young corporal who looked as if he had simply settled down on the cobbles and gone to sleep, his young face was so peaceful.

'How many, Schulze?' he asked softly.

'Twenty so far, sir. Their poor mothers!'

'They died for their country.'

'Country!' Schulze echoed mockingly.

Von Dodenburg looked up. 'What do…'

From somewhere there came a soft scream, a scream of pleasure.

'What was that?' he whispered, his body crouched, his machine pistol at the ready.

'It came from over there, sir,' Schulze answered.

'Cover me. I'm going to have a look.'

'Be careful, sir, it might be a sniper,' Schulze urged.

Cautiously, hugging the shadows that had begun to lengthen at the side of the little street, the two men advanced towards the sounds coming from a little white cottage. They were rhythmic and persistent – almost like somebody getting a bit of the other, Schulze couldn't help thinking.

Von Dodenburg came level with the door of the cottage. With the forefinger of his free hand, he indicated in eloquent dumb show that Schulze should go to the other side of the street until he was directly opposite the door. Noiselessly Schulze did as he was ordered. Von Dodenburg waited until he was in position, his machine pistol held firmly at his hip. Then he drew a deep breath and with all his strength crashed his booted foot against the wooden door. It gave immediately and he sprang back as Schulze fired a quick burst. *'Heaven, arse and twine!'* the unmistakable voice of Sergeant-Major Metzger cried in alarm.

'Good night, Marie,' Schulze breathed incredulously, *'it's the Butcher!'* Von Dodenburg, followed by the Hamburger, pushed through the door into the dark, evil-smelling room.

Sergeant-Major Metzger lay face downwards on the floor, trying frantically to pull up his trousers.

'Oh, my holy Godfather!' Schulze roared at the sight of the struggling, panic-stricken NCO. 'The Butcher with his pants down!' Then the laughter froze on his face, as he realised what the Sergeant-Major must have done. 'But you're not cured,' he yelled accusingly, 'You've given her…' He broke off suddenly. On the bed, the girl, recovering from her fright quicker than the NCO, grinned at them idiotically, her legs still wide apart just as the Butcher had left her when he had jumped from the bed in his fright.

Von Dodenburg assessed the situation at

once. 'Cover yourself,' he snapped and when the girl only reacted with a cretinous smile, he pulled down her skirt. Her smile vanished, to be replaced by a thick-lipped infantile sulk. 'Get out! Schulze, get her outside!'

Schulze grabbed hold of her and pulled her from the bed. 'Come on, Greta Garbo,' he said, 'let's go.' But, in spite of his rough manner, his voice was full of pity. 'You've given your only performance of the day.'

Outside he groped in his pocket and pulled out a squashed bar of ration chocolate, which was heavily spiked with stimulants. 'Here you are, you poor bitch. Take it and be off with you.'

The idiot girl tried to curtsey her thanks in the country manner, but failed lamentably. Munching happily on the chocolate, her mind already empty of what had just happened to her, she wandered aimlessly into the darkness.

Schulze turned back into the cottage.

The Sergeant-Major, his trousers back around his waist again, but with his flies still undone, was standing rigidly to attention in front of the enraged von Dodenburg. 'Don't you realise that we have a mission here?' he thundered. 'Not only military, but also political! We are the bringers of the New Order! Fools like you destroy the faith of the local people in us Germans. My God, man,

160

can't you understand that?'

'But she's only an idiot,' Metzger said weakly.

'*An idiot!*' von Dodenburg roared. 'Why that's even worse! What do you think the locals will make of that? The Germans enter a village, bringing with them a whole new philosophy of life, the regeneration of Europe. And what is the first thing one of their senior NCOs does – *he screws one of their idiots!*' Beside himself with rage, he swung back his hand and crashed it into the Butcher's unhappy face. The NCO staggered back against the wall, a thin trickle of blood beginning to run down his face, a look of utter disbelief in his red eyes. No one had struck him like that since he was ten years old. Sergeant-Major Metzger's whole world fell apart in that instant. He, a long-time regular soldier and the company's senior NCO, had been struck across the face like a common, shitty-arsed recruit on his first day in the Army! It just wasn't possible. But it had happened and there was worse to come for Sergeant-Major Metzger.

His eyes blazing with anger, von Dodenburg swung round to Schulze. 'Escort Metzger back to my command post. Keep an eye on him and do not hesitate to shoot if he tries to escape.'

'Yes, sir,' Schulze said with relish. 'You can rely on me.'

'As for you Metzger. You are under close arrest until we start our attack in thirty minutes. Thereafter I shall release you to open arrest.'

The Butcher attempted to stutter his thanks, but von Dodenburg cut him short. 'You will stay by my side throughout the action, do you understand?'

'Yes sir – of course, sir!'

'And one other thing.'

'Yes sir!'

'You will be carrying the flame thrower that Captain Geier brought up in the Ford. From now onwards you are my group's flame thrower operator, *Trooper* Metzger.'

Ex-Sergeant-Major Metzger stifled his groan just in time. Not only had he lost the coveted rank which had taken him ten years to reach, he had also been given what was virtually a sentence of death.

CHAPTER FIVE

The group of SS men, crouched in the mud at the canal's edge, fell flat on their faces as the searchlight swept over the still surface of the water. Like an icy white finger it traced its way across the canal, hesitated here and there, swept over their tense bodies and carried on. A moment later it went out and they were alone in the darkness.

'All right,' von Dodenburg hissed, as if the enemy were only a matter of yards away, 'get in the boat!' Awkwardly the Butcher, laden down with his flame-thrower stepped in, followed by Schulze. All along the water's edge, the others did the same. 'Move off,' von Dodenburg ordered.

Almost noiselessly they began to pull away. 'The best of luck,' the Vulture called from the bank, disappearing from sight a moment later.

Von Dodenburg shivered, he did not know whether it was fear or the sudden cold of the water. But it didn't matter. No one could see him in the darkness. Now they were exactly half way across. Up ahead he could see the dim outline of the concrete wall which disappeared into the night sky. If they were caught now, it would be a massacre, pure and simple, he thought to himself. They wouldn't have a chance.

Suddenly a green flare rushed into the night sky and hung there, apparently without motion. 'Down,' he yelled.

They stopped paddling at once. Crouched at the bottom of the boat, von Dodenburg could see Metzger's sickly-green face, his eyes wild with fear. He felt his own heart pounding wildly. Slowly the flare began to come down until, with a soft hiss, it extinguished itself in the water. Hardly able to control his voice, he said, 'All right, pull away.'

A few moments later a machine gun opened up near the wrecked bridge. They could see its white and red tracer bullets zigzagging through the darkness and hear the ricochets whining off the concrete. But whatever the enemy gun's target was, it wasn't them.

Their boat hit the concrete wall with a sudden bump. Von Dodenburg did not waste any time thanking God for their arrival. 'Get yourself into files,' he ordered softly. 'NCOs will lead. And I'll have the balls off any man who makes a noise. Get that!'

No one answered, but von Dodenburg knew that they were as well aware of the danger of their position as he was. As soon as they began to scale the concrete they would be sitting ducks once more.

Slinging his machine pistol over his shoulder and carefully adjusting the strap of his helmet, Kuno ran his hand over his equipment to check that there was nothing loose which might bang against the concrete.

He took a deep breath and, reaching up into the darkness, sought and found his first handhole. The men followed.

They lay on the top of the concrete bank wheezing like old men. At the expense of torn hands and bursting lungs, they had done it. The climb had been a nightmare, a brutal nightmare of fear and strain in the darkness but, in spite of the pain from his aching muscles and bleeding fingernails, von Dodenburg smiled weakly to himself in the darkness. They had done it without discovery. He wiped the sweat off his brow and keeping low, so as not to present too great a silhouette at the edge of the bank, he scurried over to Schwarz.

'Listen,' he whispered, cupping his hands over the other officer's ear and wrinkling his nose at Schwarz's smell. He then remembered that none of them had washed for well over twenty-four hours. 'We'll split up into two groups. The paras can't be far off now. Watch that your men don't fire at them by mistake in the darkness.'

Schwarz nodded and von Dodenburg crawled back hurriedly to his own men, going from man to man, telling each one the same, he hoped, encouraging information. 'We're almost there. We should be linking up with the paras in a few minutes.'

The SS men got wearily to their feet. In extended order, directed by the surviving NCOs' thumps and punches, for von Dodenburg had commanded that there should be no noise whatsoever, they began to plod across the wet field towards the sinister outline of Fort Eben-Emael.

165

Then, suddenly, their luck ran out. With a blinding roar, the field exploded to von Dodenburg's right. In the sudden blast of orange flame, he saw a figure blown into the air. A moment later everything was pitch-black again and a terrified voice was screaming, *'Mines, mines everywhere!'*

'Stop, stop everywhere!' von Dodenburg yelled at the top of his voice, but he was too late. Another mine exploded only ten yards away. He ducked automatically and a second later dirt and pebbles pattered down on his helmet like heavy summer rain. In the dying flame of the explosion he caught a fleeting glimpse of one of his corporals sitting on the ground, nursing the shattered stump of his right leg. Instinctively he moved to go to his aid but the corporal shouted, 'Don't come near me, sir. The things are everywhere!'

Von Dodenburg stood rooted to the spot. What should he do? From the dark outline of the first gun emplacement red flares were beginning to climb into the air. He caught the sound of an order in a language he couldn't understand. A machine gun began to chatter. It was followed by a ragged crackle of rifle fire. 'My God,' someone screamed behind him and fell to the ground. Still von Dodenburg did not move.

In the next instant Schulze had made up his mind for him. 'For Christ sake, let's get out of here, sir!' he yelled above the mounting volume of small arms fire.

'Where the hell to?'

'On top of that turret! It's the only way. We'll be in dead ground then.'

'But the mines?'

'Screw the mines!' Schulze grabbed von Dodenburg's arm. 'Come on!' The Butcher stood petrified, weighed down by the round canister of the flame-thrower. Schulze didn't hesitate. He launched a great kick at his rump. 'You too!' he yelled. *'March or croak,* that's what you always used to shout. Now, that's just what it is!'

In the light of the flares they ran across the field, straight into the deadly barrage. They ran, dropped to the ground, got up and ran some more. A mine exploded. Someone screamed. They sprang over the mutilated man and pelted on.

They hit what appeared to be a trench system. Suddenly von Dodenburg found himself facing a Belgian soldier. He recognized the Great War helmet. His father had a similar one in his study. Instinctively he fired, although the man had raised his hands in surrender. The man flew back, his stomach torn apart by the burst at such close range. The next moment he tripped and sprawled full length, his foot caught in a tangle of barbed-wire.

At the same instant Metzger pressed the trigger of his flame-thrower. A great tongue

167

of flame shot out. Twenty yards ahead two enemy soldiers were suddenly transformed into living torches. One dropped immediately, writhing frantically. The other came running on, blinded by the flames, his outstretched arms blazing fiercely. Suddenly he dropped to the ground, his black bubbling head lying in a puddle of flickering fire. Schulze dragged him to his feet. 'Come on,' he gasped. 'We're nearly there now!'

The two of them ran past an abandoned machine gun. A big black face poked up out of a hole. The thick lips muttered something in a kind of bastard French. Von Dodenburg could just make out the word 'pity'. But in the 'rage of blood' which had now possessed him he had no pity. He fired a burst at the Congolese and the black face disappeared in a welter of blood.

The way was barred by a small pillbox. At first they thought it was abandoned, but the sudden burst of fire which killed a corporal just behind von Dodenburg soon told them that it wasn't. 'Flame-thrower – quick!' Schulze snarled and pushed the Butcher forward. 'Come on, you great lover, you!'

Metzger stumbled forward and pressed the trigger. There was a soft whoosh. Flames curled round the pillbox. The metal cupola glowed dully but nothing happened.

'Give them it again!' Schulze yelled.

This time it worked. Half a dozen Belgians

came running out, coughing and blinded, their arms raised in surrender. Someone mowed them down with a single burst.

Now they were through the Belgian outer line. The firing gave way to a solitary rifle shot and the occasional angry short burst of machine gun fire. They were through the minefield too, but at a terrible cost. As they slowed down to a walk, their chests heaving, the sweat pouring down their faces, von Dodenburg could just make out the dark figures of his men on each side; and in spite of the darkness, he could see enough to tell him that he had lost half his command in the last fifteen minutes. Weakly he indicated that they should continue their advance towards the dark outline of the Fort on the horizon. Behind them in the minefield, a high hysterical voice kept calling, 'Comrades, for God's sake, don't leave me!'

The voice grew fainter and fainter until finally it died away altogether.

Fifteen minutes later they linked up with the paras. It was a totally undramatic moment. A round, rimless paratroop helmet popped up from a ditch next to the wall of the Fort and a voice said, 'What the hell took you so long?'

CHAPTER SIX

The handful of bearded, begrimed paras had set up a position between a wrecked DFS 230 glider, which had landed on top of the Fort, and a bunker which they managed to put out of action with their hollow charges. Whenever their own artillery or that of the Belgians fired on them, they fled into the bunker, but for the rest of the time they preferred to be outside. As the para sergeant in charge explained. 'It's funny in there and the men don't like it. If you listen carefully, you can hear the Belgies down below in the underground galleries. Hundreds of them there are.' He shrugged. 'The men prefer to be outside in the open even though the Belgies have brought their artillery down on us twice during the day.'

Von Dodenburg nodded his understanding. 'And what about trying to get into the galleries?' he asked.

'Not possible, Lieutenant. We've run out of hollow charges. All we've got is our machine pistols and rifles.'

'Grenades?' von Dodenburg queried. The para sergeant was exhausted. He realised that. They had pulled off one of the most amazing feats in modern warfare by landing right on top of Europe's most powerful fort and they had fought it out with an enemy who outnumbered them by the hundreds. He could not be too critical of their present lack of initiative.

'We used them in batches of three to knock out the guns in the turret below us,' the para sergeant explained. 'Some of the lads shinned along the gun barrels, hung them at the muzzles and got out of the way – fast!' Von Dodenburg rose from the slit trench. 'Sergeant, come on with me into the turret, where we can see. I want you to explain something to me.'

Crouched low, they doubled over to the bunker, where what was left of von Dodenburg's men lay sprawled out, exhausted, against the walls, while Schulze tended a dying soldier who had been shot in the lower abdomen. He turned when the two of them came in, his once ruddy face pale and drawn.

'How is he?' von Dodenburg asked.

Schulze shook his head and gave him the thumbs-down sign. 'The bullet got him in the balls, sir. I'm surprised he's survived so long.'

The young officer accepted the news without comment. The time for sympathy was past. Too many men had died in the last few hours in Assault Battalion Wotan. Now he felt utterly drained of emotion. All he could think of was to take their objective and then fall into a bed and sleep. Sleep, sleep, sleep, for ever and a day. 'Do what you can for him; make it easy,' he said to Schulze and made the gesture of pressing home the plunger of a hypodermic.

Schulze nodded. He knew what he meant. Pump a dose of morphia into the wounded boy, enough to kill him painlessly.

Von Dodenburg sat down next to the para sergeant, pulling over the candle. 'All right, sergeant, clue me in, if you would.'

Slowly, with the exaggerated precision of the overtired, the para sergeant raised his finger and began to trace in the outline of their section of the fort with his dirty forefinger in the dust on the floor. 'We're here. Below us there is a gallery, running in this direction, if I'm guessing right. Two gun emplacements run off that gallery – the one I told you we knocked out and the other which is still operating.'

'You mean Thirty?'

'Yes, I suppose it's Thirty.'

Von Dodenburg absorbed the information, staring at his own shadow flickering in the light of the candle on the wall. It seemed to take his brain a long time to digest it. Behind him the dying soldier groaned softly as Schulze plunged the needle into his arm. A moment later his head slipped to one side and his breath started to come in grunts, as if he were snoring. Schulze stretched out painfully against the wall next to the Butcher, whose exhausted face was black with smoke.

There was silence in the bunker, broken only by the dying man's breathing and the soft burr of the enemy soldiers talking far below them. Von Dodenburg jerked his head up suddenly. He had almost fallen asleep, squatting there, trying to sort out what to do next.

Wearily he rubbed his eyes, which seemed filled with large grains of sand. 'You mean that the gallery,' he began, his words slurred like those of a drunk. 'No, I mean, the gun emplacement you knocked out – it runs off the gallery below.'

The para sergeant nodded.

'Is there any way to get into that gun emplacement? Sergeant, I'm speaking to you!'

The para sergeant jerked up his head sharply. He, too, had fallen asleep, just sitting there. 'Through the gun ports – perhaps, if you had a charge.'

'How big a charge?'

'God,' the para sergeant complained, rubbing his filthy hand over his face. 'I don't know.' His eyes closed again.

Von Dodenburg grabbed him by the collar and shook him roughly. 'Sergeant, I asked you a question! *How much?*'

'A small one – a bundle of four or five hand grenades. Tied together, they might pull it off.'

Von Dodenburg relaxed his grip. The para sergeant slumped back against the wall. The next moment he was fast asleep, snoring loudly, his mouth wide open.

'Five hand grenades,' he whispered to himself. 'Just five.' Slowly a plan began to form in his mind. By dawn he wanted to be in the gallery below, ready to start the job of putting the gun emplacements out of action. He looked at the luminous dial of his watch. He had exactly ten hours left before the German Army started to cross the Meuse in force. If SS Assault Battalion Wotan did not have the guns knocked out by then, the crossing would be a massacre.

'All right, von Dodenburg,' Schwarz whispered, as the raiding party crouched on the top of the Fort, 'everything's ready.'

'Fine.' Kuno jerked at the rough-and-ready rope they had made from the seat harness of the wrecked glider. It seemed all right. He settled the bundle of grenades more comfortably. 'Ready to go.'

'Look out down there, sir,' Schulze said anxiously. 'It's going to be tricky.'

Von Dodenburg smiled. 'I will, don't fear. I'll be back to make a soldier out of you yet.'

He took a last look at the luminous dial of his watch. They had five hours at the most till dawn. 'Let her go,' he ordered, trying to hide the fear in his voice.

The men took the strain. The next moment he was over the side and they were playing out the improvised rope. Rapidly Kuno sank out of sight in the darkness. Thirty feet, forty, fifty. The wind seemed to have increased in strength. Hanging there on the face of the great Fort, he felt it tug at his body. Seventy feet. He came to a sudden stop. The thin cord tied to his wrist jerked hard. It was the agreed signal. He had reached the required depth. He must now be level with the upper gun turret, the one the paras had knocked out.

He took a deep breath and looked down. The faint silver sheen below was the Albert Canal. If he made a wrong move now, that was where he would end up. He licked his lips, reached up and caught the tough webbing of the harness with both hands.

'All right, you bastard,' he said, '*swing!*'

Slowly, almost imperceptibly at first, the makeshift rope began to move back and forth along the face of the man-made cliff. He started to gain momentum. Like a pendulum his body swung across the sheer face, striking the rough concrete with ever increasing frequency as the arc grew larger and larger. He gasped as his body was buffeted by the concrete, but he forced himself to continue, his teeth clenched with pain. Somewhere – perhaps another ten yards to his right – the silent 75 mm cannon were protruding into the night. He must secure a hold on them. *He must!*

Up above on the plateau, the SS men sweated, their eyes bulging with the strain, their heels dug deep into the soil, as the pressure on their arm muscles and burning palms mounted. They could no longer see von Dodenburg, but they could hear him as he struck the concrete time and time again.

Far below, von Dodenburg swung in a great arc through the wind which now seemed to be howling around him, grabbing at his battered body, eager to pluck him away from his fragile perch. Twice he struck his head against a piece of concrete and was only saved from losing consciousness by his helmet. Then suddenly he saw the first of the twin cannon, its muzzle splayed open where the paras had exploded their charges. Relying completely on the men above, he took his hands off the rope and grabbed for it. His nails scraped against the cold metal and then he was swinging back in the opposite direction. He tried again. And again, still to no avail! The tips of his fingers were bleeding and blunt now, without any feeling. He felt his strength ebbing rapidly. Clenching his teeth, knowing that the men could not bear the strain much longer, he came in again, the wind whistling past with almost gale-like force. He held his hands

Attack on interior of Fort Eben-Emael (May 11th 1940)

Crashed DFS glider

German para position

Route taken by Lt. V. Dodenbury

Knocked-out turret

Turret 46

Cenne Village

Albert canal

Underground system

Fort Eben-Emael

ready. The first gun loomed up. Stretching his arms to their full extent, straining with every fibre of his body, he lunged for it. His hands caught, slipped and caught again. A nail gave and he felt an electric shock of agony shoot up his arm, but he held on. Then with the last of his strength he heaved himself on to the top of the great cannon and hung there like a sack, his unseeing eyes staring down at the silver gleam of the Albert Canal far below.

For what seemed ages but, in reality, was only a matter of thirty seconds he lay there. Then he forced himself to pull the cord to signal to the men up top that he had done it. Sitting astride the gun, he began to work his way towards the turret. He reached it safely and by stretching out far to the right, he could see that the para sergeant had not lied. There was a fairly sizeable observation port there. Gingerly he reached his hand into it and felt for the far side.

He judged it to be thirty by thirty centimetres. Too tight for even the slimmest man among the survivors of 2nd Company. But give it another ten centimetres and even the bull-like Metzger would be able to get through.

He fumbled for the grenades, expertly tied together with a piece of wire by the para sergeant who had also fixed the five second fuse; like all the men who had landed on top of the Fort by glider he was a trained engineer. Biting his bottom lip, he transferred them to his left hand. One slip and they'd be gone for ever, exploding purposelessly in the Canal far below.

He managed it and by straining out, he placed them in the aperture and pulled the fuse. He clambered madly back over the first gun and the second, swung round the corner of the turret and pressed his body against the rough concrete. Just in time. The five grenades exploded with a muffled crump. A hot wind hit him in the face. Chunks of concrete sailed through the air and a few moments later he heard them hitting the water far below. He raised his head and waited for the angry shouts and the burst of machine gun fire. Nothing happened. No shouts, no bullets. Possibly the Belgies had taken the explosion for another German shell.

Cautiously von Dodenburg, suspicious of a trap, began to edge his way back to the aperture. The smoke was clearing away now to reveal the jagged shattered sides. He squeezed his head and shoulders into the enlarged hole. They went through easily and he signalled to the others to start coming down. Five minutes later the whole raiding party was crowded into the abandoned gun turret, staring round curiously in the thin blue light of Schwarz's torch.

Schwarz took the lead, machine pistol clutched at his hip. The little SS officer seemed utterly fearless. Twice he led them past posts occupied by the enemy, the light escaping from below the doors and the low murmur of tired voices indicating that Belgians were inside and awake; neither time had he shown the least sign of fear. Once a dark shape had shot out in front of them in the poorly-lit corridor, its size magnified enormously on the wall ahead by the light of Schwarz's torch. Schwarz did not seem to notice. His eyes empty of any expression, his face covered with blood and grime, he led them deeper and deeper into the interior of the great Fort, the only sound that of their own boots, now covered with their socks, and the steady throb of the air conditioning like the beat of some monstrous heart.

Suddenly Schwarz switched off his torch. 'Against the wall,' he hissed. 'Someone coming!'

Hearts beating frantically, they pressed themselves against the damp, dripping concrete, their eyes focused on the swinging arcs of light coming closer and closer. 'No firing,' von Dodenburg whispered.

Schulze, who was close behind Schwarz, clubbed his fist in anticipation. Schwarz crouched, a bayonet held tight to his side.

A great shadow swung into sight. And another. They preceded their owners like silent giants. Von Dodenburg gave a sigh of relief. Just the two of them!

'*Ici ... la bas!*' Schwarz called in his best French, just as the first man came into sight.

The Belgian corporal turned startled. '*Pardon,*' he said apologetically and clicked off the torch, as if he feared to blind Schwarz. In that same instant, the Lieutenant's bayonet slid into his side between his ribs. His mouth shot open but Schwarz's dirty hand clamped over it. His knees buckled beneath him and he sagged to the floor, the torch clattered from his hand on to the concrete.

At the same moment Schulze clubbed the other man behind the ear and, reaching up, grabbed the back of his helmet. He pulled hard. The helmet slid down, its strap falling around the Belgian's throat. Schulze's knee shot into the small of his back. With both his huge hands he tugged at the back of the helmet. The strap bit into the soldier's throat. His scream died in a sudden strangled groan. Desperately his hand clawed at the strap and tried to break the killing hold. Wriggling frantically, while Schulze held on grimly, his eyes bulging in an ecstasy of fear, he flung himself from side to side. Slowly Schulze garrotted him to death. His knees buckled as, gently, almost tenderly, Schulze lowered him to the ground. 'The poor bastard's dead,' he whispered.

While they clustered round the two dead

Belgians, running their filthy hands through their pockets in search of cigarettes, they did not see the third man, who slipped away, fearfully and noiselessly, to report the presence of these bloody begrimed invaders.

They were deep within the fort now. The chatter of its machine guns and the occasional crump of its guns were muted by the depth, whereas the sound of the Fort's machinery was getting louder by the second. Von Dodenburg held up his hand. They stopped and he pointed to a ladder directly in front of them, clamped to the cement, next to the legend DEFENSE DE FUMER. On both sides of the steel ladder there were open-doored lift shafts like the 'pater nosters' used in North Germany. 'Shell hoists going down from the magazine to the gun turret,' he explained softly.

Schulze was first off the mark. 'Let's get that bastard straight off,' he urged.

'How?'

Schulze grinned. 'Every time a machine stopped in the docks in Hamburg the workers got a coffee break. And on Monday morning after a night on the *Reeperbahn*, the machines stopped a lot.' He turned to the others crowded behind him in the shadows. 'All right, everyone grab a handful of that cement dirt there and follow me.' He suited his actions to his words and at a nod from von Dodenburg, the others started to do the same.

Grinning broadly, Schulze threw the cement dirt down inside the polished metal runner at each side of the hoist. 'Down here,' he said. 'We'll need a lot of this crap to do it. If I could get down to the engine, especially if it were gasoline, a handful of sugar and the whole thing would seize up just like that.' He clicked his thumb and forefinger loudly. 'But this lot'll do just as good once it gets into the works.'

Hurriedly man after man threw a couple of handfuls of the cement dirt into the shaft. Even Schwarz snapped out of his strange mood long enough to do the same.

Slowly the shell hoist came to a grinding halt. Schulze winked at von Dodenburg. 'Now what do you say to that, Lieutenant? Ain't that the neatest bit of sabotage you've ever seen?'

'Damn terrorist! I think I shall report you to the Gestapo. If we ever get out of here alive,' he added, but there was laughter in his voice. 'All right, you've given your star performance, Schulze. Let's get down to the rough stuff.' He gripped his machine pistol aggressively. 'That gun turret down there has got to be put out of action.'

They ran down the tunnel until they came to the stairs. At the bottom was another tunnel, dripping with the moisture that seeped through the earth, its concrete walls covered with nitre. They ran along the slippery duckboards. Twice Metzger, more ungainly than the younger men, slipped and fell. No one helped him to his feet. They all knew now that the ex-Sergeant-Major faced some serious charge or other if they ever got out of this alive.

Suddenly the tunnel curved sharply to the right. Von Dodenburg in the lead stopped just in time. A great steel door stood in front of them, sharp white light cutting into the dim yellow of the tunnel. 'Emplacement number forty-six,' he whispered.

As if to lend emphasis to his words, there was a great crash from behind the door. Although it was probably several inches thick, it trembled violently as if it were made of matchwood. The next instant the tunnel was filled with thick yellow smoke that tore at their lungs. It was followed by a monstrous clanging noise that made their hands to fly to their ears to keep the blast out. Von Dodenburg felt as if his skull were going to split apart any moment. He staggered violently against the wall and supported himself there, his body bent, the tears streaming down his face, coughing as if he would bring his very lungs up.

Schwarz, who had not received the full impact of the blast from the twin cannon in the turret, took over. 'Metzger – Schulze –

cover me, I'm going in!'

Without waiting to see if they were indeed doing so, he levelled up his machine pistol and crashed his foot against the steel door. Surprisingly enough it swung open. Obviously it was well-oiled as part of the safety measures taken against sudden flash fires.

The gunners, their heads protected by asbestos flash guards under their helmets, were grouped round the hoist. In the thick yellow smoke they were gesticulating angrily at each other, obviously placing the blame for the failure of the hoist on one another. With their ears covered by the thick asbestos, they did not hear Schwarz till it was too late.

A fat sergeant, with the yellow face of a man who had been in the fortress artillery too long, swung round and saw him. His hand reached for his pistol, but he never drew it.

Schwarz fired and the sergeant crashed against the concrete wall.

He fired again, swinging his body from left to right. The Belgian artillerymen fell where they stood, galvanised momentarily into electric action, like puppets in the hands of a mad puppet-master, before they fell to the floor. It was all over within a matter of seconds. As the chattering of the machine pistol died away, the last enemy soldier collapsed on to the floor.

Like a man mesmerised, Schwarz remained standing in the position of firing, legs astride, machine pistol clasped to his side, as if he expected the men he had just killed to rise up and he would have to begin the slaughter all over again.

'Oh, my aching back,' Schulze gasped, staring at the little officer's face, 'he's gone combat crazy! Lieutenant Schwarz is out of his mind!'

'Hold your trap,' von Dodenburg snapped. Almost gently he placed his hands on the still-smoking machine pistol and pressed it slowly downward. 'It's all right, Schwarz, it's all right.'

Schwarz shook his head. 'What's the matter?' he asked. 'What are you doing?'

'My dear Schwarz, it's all right,' von Dodenburg said soothingly.

'Of course, it's all right,' Schwarz snapped. 'What are you talking about. We've just taken Turret Forty-Six, haven't we?'

Then von Dodenburg knew that Lieutenant Kurt Schwarz was crazy, irrevocably crazy for all time.

CHAPTER SEVEN

Commandant Jottrand's face looked white even in the harsh yellow light of the naked bulb that hung in its wire cage on the ceiling. 'What did you say?' he rapped at the soldier who had brought him the news.

'There were about thirty of them,' the soldier gasped in his heavily accented French. 'All Boche.' He made the 'ch' sound like 'sch'. Major Jottrand noted that the man was a Fleming and thought again how easy the Germans had it – one great nation united behind a single leader and all speaking the same language. He, for his part, the commander of his nation's greatest fort, had to deal with two linguistic groups who hated each other bitterly and refused to function unless they were in a company composed of their own kind. What a crazy army the Belgian Army was, especially when its commander-in-chief, the King himself, was suspected of being pro-German!

'Where were they heading?'

'To Casement Forty-Six,' a voice at the door announced.

'What the devil is the meaning of this, Baer?' Commandant Jottrand snapped.

Lieutenant Baer, a Fleming himself, nodded for the private to leave; then he sprang to attention. 'Sir, I beg to report that the enemy has taken Number Forty-Six. They have destroyed the hoists and are believed to be on their way to Number Forty-Five.'

Wearily Jottrand waved for him to relax. 'I am sorry, Baer. My nerves, and the atmosphere inside here. It's been thirty-six hours since I've seen daylight,' he added by way of explanation.

'I understand, sir,' Baer snapped.

Jottrand collected himself quickly and was beginning to rap out his orders when his words were drowned by the noise of an explosion. Little bits of plaster and cement fell on his balding pate. The walls trembled and a little wave of dust swept under the door.

'You know what that was, don't you, Baer?' he said when the noise had died away.

Baer bit his lip and nodded.

'Number Forty-Five,' Jottrand said, a thin smile on his lips, as if the words gave him some kind of masochistic pleasure. 'And if we don't stop the bastards soon, thirty-six, twenty-three and seventeen will follow.' He laughed drily. 'One doesn't need to be clairvoyant to know what they're after.'

'You mean, *mon Commandant*, that the Boche are going to cross the Meuse to our north and those people below are trying to

188

put out our guns covering that sector?'

'Exactly,' Jottrand's lips tightened. 'But they're not going to do it. I fought them in the last war and beat them and I'm going to do the same in this one. Right. Where was I? I want everyone not on the guns to be formed into a provisional company – cooks, clerks, civilian cleaners too, if you can find them. Anyone who can fire a rifle, do you understand?'

'Yes sir, and then?'

Jottrand glanced at his watch hastily, 'In exactly fifteen minutes I shall ask for a barrage from the 7th Infantry Division. I am going to ask them to bring it down right on top of us. I shall swat the Boche off us like a cow does with its tail. Then we counter-attack.' Dramatically in the Latin-fashion, against which Baer's Fleming soul rebelled instinctively, he rose to his feet, every inch the traditional Gallic warrior. 'Lieutenant Baer, we must drive them out of Fort Eben-Emael. It is for the honour of the Army and the future of our nation.'

The Belgian counter-attack caught von Dodenburg's little force by complete surprise.

They had just captured Number Thirty-Six and spiked its guns by smashing their firing pins against the walls and were advancing again down the dark corridor

189

towards their next objective when the enemy machine gun opened up at pointblank range. The leading three men were cut down at once and von Dodenburg was slammed against the wall, blood pouring from his shoulder. The next instant the massed artillery of the Belgian 7th Infantry Division hit the outside of the fort. Eben-Emael rocked like a ship in a heavy sea. Fragments of concrete came tumbling down from the ceiling. The walls groaned under the strain and a fog of dust rose from the floor.

But the machine gun kept up its deadly fire. As the lead cut into them, they were bowled down the corridor, legs and arms flailing in the horrible disjointedness of violent death. Schulze yelled as a bullet whacked into his thigh and sat down. The Butcher, a neat hole drilled through the back of his hand, stood in the middle of the panic-stricken mob.

'Get down you silly bastard!' Schulze shrieked. He grabbed the Butcher's ankle, tugged hard and the ex-sergeant-major fell to the ground among the dead and dying. An instant later a hail of bullets ripped open the wall just behind where he had been standing.

Von Dodenburg shook his head to fight off the nausea that was threatening to swamp him. Ahead were a dozen enemy soldiers grouped behind a machine gun in a makeshift barricade which blocked the corridor. Beyond them every recess was lined with armed men. Their way was barred.

Still Schwarz remained on his feet, firing his machine pistol, teeth bared, murder glaring out of his eyes. A fresh explosion up above rocked the corridor. He swayed violently. Von Dodenburg grabbed his arm and nearly shrieked with pain. 'Get down, you damn fool!' he roared above the noise.

'We've got to get through,' Schwarz screamed, fitting a fresh magazine to his Schmeisser. 'The turrets – the Sixth Army!'

'I know, I know!' von Dodenburg yelled and kicked Schwarz hard on the side of the leg.

As he fell von Dodenburg flung himself on top of him, the lead cutting the air just above his head. 'Stay there,' he cried and felt a sickening thud as a slug struck the back of his helmet. 'We can't get through that barricade. They'd slaughter us.' He rolled clear and shouted at the same time. 'Everybody back up the corridor – round the bend! We'll cover you! Schwarz, start firing!'

He couldn't use his own machine pistol because of his shoulder, but he groped for his Walther and holding it awkwardly in his left hand, he joined in as Schwarz blazed a long burst at the machine gunner. Hurriedly the survivors scurried for cover, while the two officers backed down the corridor littered with their own dead, firing as they went. A few seconds later they had made it. Von Dodenburg collapsed on the ground, his head bent in exhaustion and defeat. The Belgians had stopped them after all!

The stuttering of the machine gun stopped abruptly. Above them the guns also went quiet. Von Dodenburg forced himself to sit up. He held his arm above his head in an attempt to stop the bleeding. The right side of his jacket was already soggy with blood, but the wound continued to bleed. He blinked a couple of times and stared round at his men. Of the two hundred-strong 2nd Company which had gone into action thirty-odd hours before, only thirty were still alive. The thought of the mass slaughter of those terrible hours made him feel sick. With a last effort of willpower, he pulled himself together and forced himself to think. What the devil was he going to do?

Leaning weakly against the opposite wall, the Butcher had thrown off his heavy flame-thrower and was moaning piteously, holding his wounded hand.

'Knock it off, you fat bastard,' Schulze cried. 'Those Belgies nearly blast my balls off and I'm not complaining! You and your little scratch!'

He broke off suddenly at the sound of heavy hobnailed boots grating cautiously on the concrete round the bend. Someone was

192

coming. They waited tensely, their hands gripping their weapons.

'Listen you Germans!' a hoarse voice called in excellent German. 'You'd better submit. You haven't got a chance. We'll give you five minutes to make up your mind.'

The voice was suddenly strangely muffled. 'And here's a sample of what's coming your way if you don't.'

A small round object sailed round the corner and struck the wall.

'Grenade!' someone screamed.

Frantically they flattened themselves on the ground, but the deadly little egg did not explode. Instead it lay there, giving off a thick wet cloud of what looked like smoke.

Surprisingly enough it was the Butcher who reacted to the strange phenomenon first. With his good hand he grabbed the little metal egg and flung it back the way it had come. The next moment he started to cough horribly. The man next to him, who had also breathed in the thick fumes followed suit a moment later, his body bent double as he tried to force air into his smoke-filled lungs.

Schulze looked at von Dodenburg, his face distorted with horror. *'Gas,'* he shrieked. *'It's Gas, Sir!'*

Von Dodenburg felt a thrill of fear run through him. *'Gas!'* he echoed. *'They wouldn't dare!'* But the faint smell of bitter

193

almonds told him they would. He had left his own gas mask behind on the plateau before he had been lowered to the first turret. But most of the men had their corrugated metal gas mask containers fixed to their belts. 'Take out your masks,' he ordered, realising that they would survive while he would be slowly choked to death by the fumes.

'I haven't got one!' someone screamed in panic.

'I haven't either.'

'I've got a bottle of cognac in my container!'

From all sides the scared voices confirmed that the men had done exactly what their predecessors had done during the Polish campaign – they had dumped the heavy gas masks as an unnecessary burden and filled the container with extra food, personal possessions or drink.

'All right, all right.' Von Dodenburg held up his good hand to stop the panic. He knew that if he didn't calm them, they would break completely; then nothing could stop them surrendering. He remembered what his father's battalion had done when the chemicals had begun to give out in their primitive masks during an Allied gas attack in 1918. 'There's no reason to panic. There's a way out. All of you, get a rag. Anything big enough to make a mask to cover your mouth. *Hurry!*'

He suited his actions to his words by tearing a strip from his shirt. The next instant he ripped open his flies and poised himself over the rag, his legs astride. 'Now piss on it!' He picked up the sodden rag and without hesitation tied it around his mouth with one hand.

Urgently they followed his example. Frantic with fear they tore at their clothing. Flies were jerked open as they crouched and urinated over the handkerchiefs or bits of shirt, and wrapped them around their mouths in panic-stricken haste.

Just in time. The first of the bombs came whizzing into their part of the corridor. Almost before it rolled to a stop, Schwarz kicked it neatly back the way it had come. But there were more.

In spite of the improvised masks, the thick fumes started to creep into their lungs. As more and more of the deadly little eggs landed in their midst, masking their feet in a thick white fog, their lungs began to sting. Von Dodenburg coughed. It felt as if a red-hot rod had been poked into them. His eyes smarted. Tears started to blind him. He ripped at his collar. He was choking. The fog rose higher. A man screamed and before anyone could stop him, he had broken away and was pelting round the bend towards the enemy.

'He didn't make it. The machine gun chattered. He flung up his hands despairingly and skidded to a stop. For one long moment he stood there before he started to sink into the thick white fog.

Another man collapsed to his knees, his mask askew, a thin bloody foam forming on his lips where he had bitten them in his last desperate attempt not to breathe in the killing fumes. Slowly but inevitably his knees began to sink to the ground. Von Dodenburg watched with horrified fascination, as if mesmerised by the scene, the coughs racking his body, tears streaming down his cheeks. He was going himself now. He could feel his knees start to buckle beneath him. He was as weak as a child. He grasped his throat and tried to stop the gas penetrating his lungs. A great red night threatened to overcome him. All around him they were sinking now. As if in a slow-motion film, the machine pistol slipped from Schwarz's nerveless fingers and clattered to the floor. Above his mask, Schwarz's crazy eyes rolled upwards. His knees started to give. Slowly he, too, began to sink into the fog.

Suddenly a well-remembered Prussian voice penetrated the red mist which threatened to submerge von Dodenburg. It was far, far away. But there was no mistaking it. A small figure, with a blood-stained bandage around his head, thrust past the dying officer. He looked ghastly in his black mask with the steamed-up eye piece. He dropped the cane he was carrying and seized the flame-thrower the top of which stuck up above the grey-white fog. With frenzied fingers, he ripped off what was left of his torn jacket and flung it to the floor. As the great blast of cool, clean air streamed in from somewhere and the mixed bunch of masked paras and SS men stormed through the ranks of the gassed 2nd Company, the Vulture strapped on the flame-thrower. He waved his hand. The sign for forward/attack.

While the men on the floor gulped in great breaths of fresh air, the Vulture swung round the bend, followed by the survivors of the bombardment on the surface of Fort Eben-Emael. He pressed the trigger and a vicious red flame shot out and wrapped itself round the barrier. He fired again. The machine gun glowed a dull red. The corridor echoed with the Belgians' screams. But the Vulture showed no mercy. He fired again. The survivors were fleeing up the corridor now, clawing at each other frantically to escape the all consuming flame, while behind them the bodies of the gunners fused to their weapon, grotesquely distorted by the tremendous heat, shrivelled up like 'little black pigmies', as the Army demonstration sergeant had predicted so confidently in what seemed another age.

CHAPTER EIGHT

It was zero four hundred. In another thirty minutes it would be dawn, the time set by Captain Geier for their last attack on the two remaining turrets. Now the corridor, littered with bodies of their own men and the charred corpses of the enemy, was silent save for the occasional crack and whine of bullets, fired by some cunning Belgian sniper, doing some nice deflection shooting further up the passage. But with little success; the men of 2nd Company, Assault Battalion Wotan were sprawled out on the floor, recovering from the exertions of the last few hours.

Schulze thrust in another plug and watched carefully as it began to fill with blood from the wound in von Dodenburg's shoulder. It was the third he'd made from the spare pair of underpants, which he had been carrying in his gas mask container, together with several blue-coloured packets of contraceptives, type VULKAN 'guaranteed to withstand the most severe eruption', as the makers claimed. 'Just in case, sir,' he had explained. 'Clean drawers and a Parisian and you're well away, fit for any fighting situation.'

'I think the bleeding's stopping now, sir.'

'Thank you, Schulze. I think you're right.'
The Vulture, his face still red where the mask had been, a rim of black across the ridge of his monstrous nose making him look even more like his namesake, pushed his way through to them. 'How's it going, von Dodenburg?' he asked, his only concern the fact that a useful officer might be unable to take part in the last stage of the operation.

'Fair, sir. The bleeding's beginning to stop.'

'Fine.' The Vulture indicated that Schulze was no longer needed.

Painfully Schulze rose to his feet and left the two officers.

The Vulture shivered in the dank cold of the corridor. He was still without his jacket. Vaguely von Dodenburg noted how thin his arms were; looked like those of an under-nourished child. But, in spite of his head wound and his frail body, he showed no sign of exhaustion. Almost immediately he launched into his plan for the final stage, while von Dodenburg listened the best he could, his head threatening to burst at any moment.

The Butcher, squatting miserably on his own in the darker part of the corridor, watched the two officers closely. The two of them would soon decide his fate, if he managed to survive the mess they were in.

He blinked a couple of times and fought back the tears of self-pity which came to his eyes. 'After all I've done for the shits,' he thought wretchedly. 'Built up the company for them, got myself wounded and now they want to throw me on the scrapheap or worse.' He sniffed and felt in the Vulture's discarded jacket in case the CO had left one of his fine cigars in there.

The Vulture hadn't but Metzger's hand fell on something else – a photograph which the CO had obviously had in his possession a long time; its edges were crumpled and worn, as if he had kept it in his wallet or identity document. Slowly and without any great curiosity, he turned it over.

What he saw made him sit bolt upright. There were two men looking out at him from the yellowing photograph, smiling with creased brows as if they were looking into the sun. The Vulture was obviously a lot younger when it had been taken; he still had most of his hair. But it was not the men's faces which made Metzger's little red eyes nearly pop out of his head, nor their completely naked bodies; it was the blatant obscenity of what they were doing to each other.

He cast a quick glance at the little Captain crouched next to von Dodenburg. Now he knew why the CO was not married; it was not just wholehearted devotion to duty. Now he knew too what the Vulture did on those semi-annual leaves to Berlin, from which he returned with dark circles under his eyes, morose, silent and drained of his usual energy.

The Butcher was not a very intelligent man. Most of those who knew him well thought, indeed, that he was very stupid. But in spite of his lack of brainpower, he realised immediately that he had a greater treasure in his possession than – mentally, he sought for a comparison – than the handwritten copy of the fabled first version of *Mein Kampf*, which the Führer had composed during his imprisonment in Landsberg Prison.

He realised, with a warm glow of relief, that with the photograph in his possession, he was saved. He stuffed it in his jacket pocket and patted it a couple of times to reassure himself that it was safely stowed away.

It was nearly dawn now and time for the last attack. Schulze had finished checking the magazine of his Schmeisser. He had taken off his jacket and was pulling off the last shreds of his ruined shirt.

Idly, savouring the last moments of inactivity before the killing started again, von Dodenburg watched him. Suddenly Schulze turned his body and revealed his back. It was covered with ugly, red weals.

'Where did you get those marks?' von Dodenburg asked curiously.

'They're nothing, sir,' he said hesitantly.

'Nothing indeed! Where did you get them?'

'From a radiator – in Neuengamme Concentration Camp.'

'*What* did you say?'

Schulze hesitated. How could he explain that miserable, terrible summer of 1938 when the Gestapo had broken into his father's illegal printing shop in Barmbek and found the anti-Nazi leaflets? The silly old bastard with his socialist principles and crappy leaflets about the rise in the price of butter under the Nazis! Who in hell cared? But the Gestapo did. Within the hour, he had been arrested with the rest of the family.

They had come to arrest him at the docks, four of them in ankle-length leather coats, with their hats pulled down over their faces like detectives in the movies. As soon as they had got him in the dark-green police Mercedes, all four of them had begun to beat him up in a stolid, dogged, routine sort of way.

The beating had been nothing new to him. It was the usual way the Hamburg police made their arrests, and it wasn't the first time he had experienced this *erste Abreibung*. The gigantic cops who manned the *Reeperbahn's* notorious St David's Police Station had given him the same going-over a couple of times when he had been dragged in there on a charge of being drunk and disorderly during one of his periodic pay-day binges.

But what had happened to him next out in Neuengamme had been completely different – the black-clad guards and their black alsatians which would bite the balls off a prisoner at their command, the beatings with the whips made of bull pizzles, Sergeant Lohmeyer, the one-legged veteran of the 1923 Munich Putsch, who made the prisoners open their mouths so that he could piss in them when he was drunk, which was most of the time. How did he explain that?

'Go on, Schulze,' von Dodenburg prompted, 'What happened?'

'Two of the bastards held me against a radiator when it was red-hot. Fifty degrees they said it was. The bastards – wish I had 'em here now with this here machine pistol in my hands.'

'But didn't you report them? Torture is illegal. Good grief man, things like that can't happen in the Third Reich!'

Schulze looked cynically at the young officer's earnest face. 'You don't know the half of it, sir,' he said. 'I could tell you things about our well-organized Greater German state…' He broke off suddenly and shrugged. 'But no one would believe me. They'd say it could never happen.'

Von Dodenburg knew he was skating on thin ice, but his outraged sense of justice drove him on. 'What do you mean no one would believe you? Of course they will, if you're telling the truth! Who did that terrible thing to your back, Schulze?'

Something snapped in the big, good-humoured Hamburger. He leaned forward. 'I'll tell you, sir, who did it. A big fat perverted bastard, who calls himself an old fighter, possessor of the "Blood Order", who can only get it up when he beats some bastard of a prisoner!'

'But what formation did he belong to?' von Dodenburg persisted. Schulze laughed bitterly. 'What formation? Hell, sir, the arsehole wears the same uniform as we do!' He looked the shocked officer in the eyes. 'He's in the SS.'

Von Dodenburg's mouth fell open. 'Impossible,' he breathed almost inaudible. *'Impossible.'*

And then the Vulture was calling them together for the last attack.

'Go,' Captain Geier yelled.

'Go!' Lieutenant von Dodenburg shrieked.

They charged forward up the corridor into the unknown, screaming hoarse obscenities.

The Belgians were waiting for them. The first SS man crumpled like a deflated paper bag. Another screamed and clapped his hands to his eyes. But the Belgians were no match for the SS. They stormed the makeshift barrier at the end of the corridor within seconds.

Drunk with blood lust and eager to die, they stabbed and cut on all sides. Belgian hand grenades burst with hollow detonation. Red-hot shards of metal hissed through the air. Men cursed. Men screamed. Men died.

Lieutenant Schwarz booted open the door of what looked like a supply room. Splay-legged he sprayed the terrified men crouching among the bins, screaming crazily. They went down like summer wheat before the harvester.

They stormed into the first turret. The gunners, horrified at this crazy pack of filthy, bloody, ragged giants, put up their arms. They shot two and the rest were beaten and kicked out of the way while a volunteer loaded two shells into the cannon and pulled the lanyard. The great cannon exploded with a tremendous roar, a neat split down the length of its barrel. When the smoke cleared, the Belgians were slumped against the wall, bleeding from nose and ears. On the floor, the volunteer lay unconscious, both his hands neatly severed. All that was left were two bleeding stumps. They left him to bleed to death and ran on.

Geier, still carrying the bulk of the flame-thrower, pressed the trigger for the last time. It belched at a group of Belgians trying to make a stand. The flame rushed down the corridor and swept them away as if they had never been there. When they ran on this time, their hobnails crunched over what sounded like cinders.

Schulze howled like a mad dog. He threw one of his captured Belgian egg grenades into a group of the enemy fleeing up the corridor. It exploded in their midst and they were bowled over, screaming horribly. He trampled over them.

Then they burst into the last turret where the gunners surrendered immediately. Now the *blutrausch* had evaporated. They quietly disarmed the Belgians and with hands that fluttered uncontrollably, they indicated that the prisoners should line up against the opposite wall. They weren't even kicked to hurry them up.

Von Dodenburg and Schwarz summoned up enough strength to unscrew the guns' firing pins and smash them. Then they, too, slumped on the floor with the rest. Drained completely of energy, friend and foe crouched there in a heavy silence, broken only by their harsh breathing, heads bent as if in defeat.

And to the north, unseen by the handful of exhausted survivors who had made it possible, the first soldiers of General Reichenau's Sixth Army began to cross the Canal. At first a company, then a battalion, the men fearful that the great guns they knew the Fort contained would open up on them when they were in mid-stream. But the cannon remained silent. A regiment followed. It became a division, then a corps. As far as the eye could see, the flat countryside was one great moving mass of field-grey. The great triumphant dash into France could begin.

Fort Eben-Emael was in German hands.

CHAPTER NINE

A strange sound woke them from their apathetic daze.

'What was that?' someone said.

'It's a trumpet – an infantry trumpet,' the Vulture said.

He got slowly to his feet and stumbled past the Belgian prisoners to peer through the observer's aperture.

'They're surrendering!' he breathed excitedly. 'There are German troops down there and white flags, white flags everywhere. The Belgians have given up!'

Now they could hear thin cheers rising from below.

'Come on,' Geier said, rolling down his sleeves to cover his thin arms and ordering his last wisps of hair.

'There'll be photographers. They mustn't miss SS Assault Battalion Wotan!'

A heavy silence lay over the plateau, broken only by the awkward stumbling steps of the brown-clad Belgians coming out to surrender – hundreds of them, led by their bitter-faced defeated commander, Major Jottrand.

The smell of death and destruction lay everywhere. It was a curious smell, redolent of long-locked-up casements, cement dust, explosives and blood.

Von Dodenburg walked over to the Belgian prisoners who were already laying their dead in long files under the supervision of a young German infantryman, his field-grey uniform neat and unstained. He looked at the bodies. They had fought well, but they had had no real purpose, no will to conquer, to be triumphant.

A country's greatness depends on the readiness of its people to sacrifice themselves for a cause but their comrades had not been prepared to do that because they had no real cause. They had remained mechanics, farmers, shopkeepers in uniform and could not expect greatness. For in the final analysis all they wanted was to earn a nice comfortable living. They had no dream.

'Sir,' it was Schulze. 'We're ready.'

Together they limped back to where the survivors of the company were arranged in a rough double line. Von Dodenburg tugged at his helmet and squared his shoulders while Schulze moved back into the line. 'Watch it,' he snapped.

Their positions stiffened. 'Company – company, *attention!*' he yelled, while the hundreds of field-greys crowded around the great fort stared in amazement.

As if they were back on the parade ground at the Adolf Hitler Barracks, the blood-stained, exhausted young giants snapped to attention, their hands stiffly held down their sides, their bodies rigid, their eyes staring into the distance.

Lieutenant von Dodenburg whirled round and marched stiffly towards where Captain Geier was waiting for him, his skinny little body erect. At the top of his voice he made his report. 'Second Company, SS Assault Battalion Wotan present! One hundred and sixty-four casualties! Twenty men on parade, *sir!*' In the momentary silence while Geier mustered the filthy blood-stained young officer in his ragged uniform, an unknown voice among the crowd of *Wehrmacht* soldiers said in a mixture of contempt and admiration, 'Can you beat it? Having a shitty parade in the middle of a battle. Ain't that typical of the SS!'

In his cavalry officer fashion, the Vulture touched his cane, which Schulze had been sent to retrieve, to his smoke-blackened helmet. 'Thank you, von Dodenburg. Please tell the men, "thank you" and then march them off.'

Von Dodenburg saluted, swung round and said formally, 'The CO wishes to thank you.' Without a pause, he raised his voice and ordered 'Right turn.'

As one they stamped round.

Von Dodenburg stared at them in admiration. Where in the world would one find troops like them – veterans already, men with an unquenchable desire to fight and win?

'Second Company – march!'

With Geier and von Dodenburg at their head, the survivors swung down the hill towards the village of Canne, past the truck which 6th Army had sent to pick them up. The driver pushed back his helmet and shook his head in wonder.

'A song,' von Dodenburg yelled, 'one – two!' And they burst into that song which would soon make the whole of the Old Continent shiver in anticipation and fear:

'Clear the streets, the SS marches
The storm-columns stand at the ready.
They will take the road
From tyranny to freedom.
So we are ready to give our all
As did our fathers before us.
Let death be our battle companion
We are the Black Band...'

Then they were gone.

AFTERMATH

'My poor brave soldiers!'
Adolf Hitler to Major Geier, 21 June, 1940.

May, 1940, flew by in one great glorious dream, punctuated by the dressing of their wounds and painful probings carried out by respectful doctors, who were supervised by a team of specialists sent from the Berlin *La Charité* Hospital by Reichsführer Himmler himself. Every morning the newspaper of the SS, *Das Schwarze Korps,* bore huge banner headlines, underlined in red, screaming the news of victory after victory. It seemed to von Dodenburg, impatiently waiting for his wound to heal, that the brassy blare of trumpets on the radio, heralding yet another special announcement and another great triumph in the West, never ceased. In the bitter years to come, he would always remember that May as the happiest month of his whole life.

It was a happiness shared by the other survivors of the 2nd Company. A week after they had been delivered to the Cavalry Hospital in Heidelberg the Vulture had ordered champagne for every one. It must have cut a large hole in his pay for that month, but the little Company Commander insisted on celebrating. He had been promoted to the rank of major and been given command of the SS Assault Battalion.

The Butcher, too, took the opportunity offered by the promotion party to talk confidentially with the new Major. At first the Vulture denied his hesitant accusations hotly, but when the Butcher produced the photograph, his thin shoulders slumped a little in defeat and, looking up at Metzger, asked him what he wanted for his silence. 'My old rank, sir, that's all.'

'You realise you'll be the most hated man in the company – perhaps in the whole battalion? The survivors will know about you?' The Butcher nodded numbly. 'I know that, sir. But I want my rank back.

The Vulture smiled cynically. 'Of course, I realise how important that is to you – and you shall have it. Perhaps, you can come and visit me in my quarters one of these evenings.' Deliberately he ran his claw-like hand over the Butcher's big beefy paw.

The Butcher flushed hotly and drew his hand away quickly. Geier's cynical smile deepened. 'We all have to pay for our little vanities and pleasures, my dear Metzger.' But behind the mask of his face, his cold brain was racing. Metzger was a danger to his career; he must not be allowed to survive the next campaign. Somehow or other he must kill him and destroy that damn fool photo of himself and Beppo, the Italian fisherboy, the one great love of his life.

Schulze occupied his time in hospital with

more mundane matters. Once von Dodenburg visited him in his ward and remarked on the pencil marks on the wall behind his head. 'They're the score-marks,' Schulze explained cheerfully.

'Score-marks?'

'Yes, sir. The nurses. When they come to dress my wound, they can't help but see my other broken bone, and being patriotic German girls they feel they have to sacrifice themselves for the cause. Two more to go and I've had the lot except that male nurse.' Schulze gave a mock frown. 'But I don't know about him. He's really not my type.'

Von Dodenburg shook his head. 'Haven't you got anything else in your head than that?'

'It's not in my head that I want it, sir,' he replied easily. 'That starts you thinking. And if you don't watch out, you're doing stuff to yourself. And as my old man used to say to me when I was a lad, that can lead to your teeth falling out and hair growing on your palms.'

'God knows what the Führer would say if he realised that he had such veterans in the SS as you!'

Three weeks later the Master of all Europe from Poland to the English Channel found out. On 20 June, as the French began to lay down their arms, a full colonel arrived at the hospital, bearing personal orders from the Führer that they should attend him at the Forest of Compiègne near Paris, where he was due to sign the French surrender treaty.

Instantly the whole hospital was in an uproar. Uniforms had to be found and fitted. Wound medals and badges of rank had to be fixed on. A team of doctors was formed to accompany them in case anything went wrong with their wounds during the flight and the presentation; and the colonel from the Führer's Headquarters had to be kept at the hospital so that he could brief them on protocol. But finally they were ready to be driven out to the Heidelberg military air strip for the flight to France, with Schulze hobbling to the staff car convoy at the very last moment, buttoning up his flies as he did so.

'What the devil kept you?' von Dodenburg snapped.

'I decided not to bother about the male nurse,' Schulze replied happily.

'But I did get the sister – in the broom cupboard!'

It was a beautiful warm June afternoon when they arrived at the Forest of Compiègne. The sun beat down on the ancient trees, which cast pleasant shadows on the glade where the sweating *Wehrmacht* engineers had finally positioned the old *wagon-lit* the tangible symbol of Germany's greatest defeat. In it the Kaiser's representatives had been forced to sign the armistice in 1918 under Marshal Foch's cold-blooded threats. The engineers had torn down the wall of the museum which had housed it and pushed it into the exact spot where the little Gallic cock of a Marshal had had his greatest triumph at 5 am on that terrible 11 November.

Now it was the turn of the man who had been a humble corporal at that moment. Wounded and blinded in a Munich hospital, he had cried when he heard the news and had sworn an oath that he would avenge Germany's disgrace, if needs be, by force of arms. In exactly six weeks he had done what it had taken the Allies four years to do. France was beaten and the British had fled the continent, taking with them only what they could carry.

At 3.15 pm precisely, that same ex-corporal arrived in his big black Mercedes. With him were those men who had helped him to achieve his revenge. At the head of this brilliant cavalcade of high-ranking officers and party leaders, he strode into the glade, his step springy, his head raised in triumph.

Standing rigidly to attention just behind Geier, von Dodenburg saw how his attention was suddenly caught by the great granite block which the French had erected twenty-two years before to celebrate their victory. He stopped and then slowly walked up to it and read its infamous inscription, which von Dodenburg knew as if it had been branded on his heart by fire.

HERE ON THE ELEVENTH OF NOVEMBER 1918 SUCCUMBED THE CRIMINAL PRIDE OF THE GERMAN EMPIRE – VANQUISHED BY THE FREE PEOPLES WHICH IT TRIED TO ENSLAVE.

The young officer watched his Führer closely. Slowly Hitler stepped back a pace. He snapped his hands on his hips, arched his shoulders and planting his booted feet wide apart, he stared up at the granite block in a magnificent gesture of contempt.

Von Dodenburg felt at that moment that he could never betray Germany's man-of-destiny. He knew he must follow this man to the very end.

A plump man with receding hair, who had the look of a middle-weight boxer gone to seed, stepped close to the Führer and whispered something in his ear. It was Bormann, Hess's secretary, who took care of matters of protocol. Hitler listened and then nodded.

Turning, he advanced on the little group of SS men drawn up at the side of the glade.

Major Geier presented the company.

Hitler thanked him in a hoarse military manner. For one long moment he stared at their young faces. To von Dodenburg it seemed like an eternity. Then his dark eyes softened. They grew liquid and filled with genuine tears. 'Only twenty left, Major Geier?' he asked in a broken voice.

'Yes, My Leader,' Geier snapped.

The Führer shook his head to get rid of the tears. 'My poor brave soldiers,' he whispered, almost to himself. 'Poor brave soldiers!'

He pulled himself together and, although time was short, insisted on shaking each one by the hand, looking up directly into their eyes with his own piercing gaze. Von Dodenburg could hardly repress the shudder of delight, pride, fear – a whole range of emotions, which he would never be able to express. All he knew was that that fleeting instant, when Adolf Hitler took his hand and stared into his face, made everything seem worthwhile.

The rest of the brief ceremony passed in a haze – the decorations, the words of praise, the Führer's flattering reference to 'my SS, the *élite* of the nation', his promise of the 'great days still to come'. And then the great man was gone.

They caught one last glimpse of him, seated proudly in the chair that Foch himself had occupied in the *wagon-lit* in 1918, waiting for the French delegation to arrive.

Just as they had started to get into the cars which would take them back to Orly Field for the flight to Heidelberg, the French arrived. They looked beaten, humiliated and shabby, in spite of their fine powder-blue uniforms, like representatives of a decadent civilization, which deserved to perish and knew it. Von Dodenburg gave them one quick glance, then turned his gaze away hastily. The French weren't pleasant to look at.

'Morning soldiers!' Major Geier yelled.

'Morning Major!' the new draft sang out the traditional reply.

Major Geier, mounted on the rostrum, slapped his cane against the side of his immaculately polished boots and said, 'Soldiers, my name is Geier, which, I am told, aptly suits my appearance.' He stroked his monstrous nose, as if to emphasize his point, just as he had done on that cold winter's morning when he had welcomed the January draft.

But if the cadre of his new 2nd Company remembered that morning, their faces did not show it – Schwarz, with the silver medal and the Iron Cross, first class, decorating his small chest, his dark eyes heavy and staring with incurable madness; Sergeant-Major Metzger, bearing his old rank to the complete astonishment of the survivors, a new cunning in his little red eyes; Schulze, a sergeant now, and the only 'other ranker' in the whole Battalion to have been decorated

220

with the Iron Cross, first class, for his courage in the middle of the minefield; and a handful more of the survivors of the 2nd Company, who had been fit enough to return to full duty.

'At present, as you can see,' the Vulture was saying to the attentive draft, 'my rank is that of a lowly major. But my father was a general and before this war is over, I promise you I shall be General Geier too.' He pointed his cane at them. 'And do you know how I shall do it...?'

Von Dodenburg turned his attention to the new draft. Their eager young faces were as yet unblemished by the marks of war. They were green – very green. But they were the best material Germany could offer in this autumn of the tremendous year of victory, 1940, every man a volunteer.

Nor were they drawn solely from the Reich this time. Among their ranks were youths from neutral Sweden and Switzerland, as well as from those countries, which up to recently had been Germany's bitter enemies – Flemings from rural Belgium, slim blonds from Norway and Denmark, sturdy Dutch farmers' sons. For von Dodenburg they were the tangible symbols of the New Europe; the youthful standard-bearers of a new era in the Continent's long history. As his eyes travelled along their ranks, he imagined them as a new kind of Imperial Guard, not dedicated to the service of one country as Napoleon's had been, but to that of the Germanic New Order which would rejuvenate the weary, decadent old Continent, give it new energy, new blood, new purpose so that once again it would take its rightful place as the arbiter of the world's fate. This was the morning of a new era. *Young Europe was on the march and nothing could stop them!*

Up on the rostrum, the Vulture toyed with his new Knight's Cross, the first to be awarded in the whole of the Division. 'Soldiers,' he rasped, 'I do not ask you to love me. I do not ask you to respect me. All I ask from you is that you obey my orders with unquestioning obedience.' His eyes swept their ranks. 'And God help any one of you, soldier, NCO or officer who fails to do exactly that.' His voice rose harshly. *'Soldiers, I welcome you to SS Assault Battalion Wotan!'*